TROPIC OF VIOLENCE

Nathacha Appanah

TROPIC OF VIOLENCE

A Novel

Translated from the French by
Geoffrey Strachan

Graywolf Press

First published in the French language as *Tropique de la violence* by Editions Gallimard, Paris, in 2016. First published in English by MacLehose Press, an imprint of Quercus, London, in 2018.

This publication is made possible, in part, by the voters of Minnesota through a Minnesota State Arts Board Operating Support grant, thanks to a legislative appropriation from the arts and cultural heritage fund. Significant support has also been provided by Target, the McKnight Foundation, the Lannan Foundation, the Amazon Literary Partnership, and other generous contributions from foundations, corporations, and individuals. To these organizations and individuals we offer our heartfelt thanks.

MINNESOTA STATE ARTS BOARD

CLEAN WATER LAND & LEGACY AMENDMENT

TARGET.

INSTITUT FRANÇAIS ROYAUME-UNI

This book is supported by the Institute Français (Royaume Uni) as part of the Burgesse programme.

Published by Graywolf Press
250 Third Avenue North, Suite 600
Minneapolis, Minnesota 55401

www.graywolfpress.org

Published in the United States of America

ISBN 978-1-64445-024-6

2 4 6 8 9 7 5 3 1
First Graywolf Printing, 2020

Library of Congress Control Number: 2019949950

Cover design: Jeenee Lee Design

Cover art: SUPERFLEX, *Kwassa Kwassa* (film still). Used with the permission of SUPERFLEX and 1301PE.

TRANSLATOR'S NOTE

The action in this novel takes place partly in France, but mainly on the French island of Mayotte, also known as Mahoré, which lies among the Comoros Islands in the Mozambique Channel. The principal city, Mamoudzou, is situated on the main island, Grande-Terre. This is linked by a ferry to the lesser island, Petite-Terre, where the town of Dzaoudzi is situated. Politically, Mayotte is a *département* of France.

In her French text, Nathacha Appanah uses a number of words from the local language, Shimaore, which I have retained in this English translation, including *kwassa-kwassas*, the name given to the frail vessels that bring refugees to Mayotte; *muzungu*, a foreigner; *banga*, a corrugated iron hut; *bacoco*, an old man; *bweni*, a woman; *sousou*, a prostitute; *mourengué*, the traditional style of bare-fisted fighting; *cadi*, a Muslim judge; and *caribou*, welcome.

To convey a further flavor of the language of some of the young people on Mayotte who appear in this novel, I have borrowed a few words from British-English slang, for example "Don" or "Daddy" for gang leader, "homeboys," and so on.

The original French text contains a number of quotations from and references to the book *L'enfant et la rivière*, by Henri Bosco, first published in 1953, in which the narrator, Pascalet, rescues and befriends Gatzo, a boy held captive by gypsies. A spirited English translation by Gerard Hopkins, *The Boy and the River*, was published in 1956. Where Nathacha Appanah quotes from Bosco's original text I have borrowed some sentences from this translation.

I am indebted to a number of people, including the author, for their advice and assistance in the preparation of this translation. My thanks are due in particular to Nathacha Appanah, Georgia de Chamberet, June Elks, Pierre Sciama, Simon Strachan, and Susan Strachan.

G.S.

"There?" I asked.

"There," he answered. "It's a beautiful country."

Henri Bosco, The Boy and the River

TROPIC OF VIOLENCE

Marie

You must believe me. In the place where I'm speaking to you from, lies and pretense are pointless. When I look into the depths of the sea, I can see men and women swimming there with dugongs and coelacanths, I can see dreams caught up in the weeds and babies asleep there, cradled in giant clam shells. In the place where I'm speaking to you from, this country looks like a handful of incandescent dust and I know it will only take some little thing for it all to go up in flames. I can't remember everything about my life for all that subsists here is the edge of things and the echo of what no longer exists.

Here's what I remember.

I'm twenty-three and the train's coming, blue and dirty. I'm leaving the valley where I grew up, where I was a frail, lost little thing, overwhelmed by the mountains. I've had enough of seeing the winter darkness flooding in over houses and faces. I've had enough of the musty smell of the morning air, I've had enough of my mother who's losing her mind, and never stops talking and spends the whole day listening to records of Barbara.

I'm twenty-four and I'm still just as frail and lost. I finish my training as a nurse in a big city. I share a vast flat with three other students and on some nights the noise, the light and the talk are like a black hole swallowing me up. I have lots of lovers; I fuck like a woman I don't recognize, who rather disgusts me. I'll go with one, leave him, then go with him again, and no one says a thing. I choose to work nights at the hospital. Sometimes I'll lie down on beds that have been stripped and are still warm, trying to imagine what it would be like to be someone else.

I'm twenty-six and I meet Chamsidine who's a nurse like me. The first time he speaks to me something odd happens. My heart, the organ firmly located in my chest, sinks down into my plexus, and starts to beat right there in the middle of me, at my center. Chamsidine has broad shoulders and can carry an adult man in his arms without batting an eyelid. When he smiles I have to take deep breaths so as not to go weak at the knees. When he utters his great peals of laughter I feel my vagina opening like a flower and I clamp my legs tightly together. All the female nurses are a little besotted with this big black man who comes from an island called Mayotte, but I don't know why I'm the one he chooses one night when we're on duty. I'm shy with this man. I'm twenty-six and I fall. He talks to me as if he'd been waiting for me for a long time. He tells me stories and legends from his homeland, talks about things that happened to him when he was little, times when he did this and when his mother told him that and I just listen in rapt silence. It seems to me as if Cham's life has been spent on an island of children, green and fertile, an island where all is play from dawn to dusk, where all the aunts, cousins, and sisters are just so many kindly mothers. When I'm getting up in the morning amid the hubbub of the city I think about that country.

I'm twenty-seven and I marry. I don't remember my dress but I remember my mother waiting with me outside the town hall. The wind's so strong that it's blown over the box shrubs in pots set out across the paved courtyard. Chamsidine's late. My mother says to me *Watch out Marie, men are all the same.* Then Cham appears, running and laughing.

I'm twenty-eight and I'm living on Mayotte, a French island tucked away in the Mozambique Channel. We rent the first floor of a house in the commune of Passamainti, a few miles from the capital, Mamoudzou. I work as a night nurse at the district hospital. Chamsidine works in the hospital at Dzaoudzi, across the water on the island of Petite-Terre. Every morning when I come off duty at six o'clock, whatever my night has been like, however hard that spell of duty has been, I walk slowly, lightly, very lightly, into the morning. I walk down the hill and I know the little girl will be waiting for me. She's covered in copper-colored dust, her hands and feet are sturdy, like those of a workman, her hair dirty and gray. She waits for me with a smile. Before going off duty I've picked up something lying about at the canteen, a package of cookies, an orange or an apple. Since I've been working here a strange relationship has grown up between her and me. I stop in front of her, she smiles, and I give her what I have to give. She never says anything to me, no good morning, no thank you, no *au revoir.* She holds out her hand quickly, I sense that she doesn't want to look as if she's begging, and besides, she looks me in the eye, never at what I put in her hand. She closes her fingers around it at once and puts her hand behind her back. Her smile grows a little broader. This is a tiny bonus to match the trifle I've given her. I don't know if she understands French. I've never told her my name and I've never asked for hers. Maybe she lives in the corrugated iron shack I can glimpse among the stunted trees, up on the hillside. Maybe she lives hidden in the woods like many of the families of illegal immigrants. Maybe what I give her will be shared among several people. Maybe. But I don't think much about all that. I do what I do, it costs me nothing, it doesn't oblige her to be grateful, it hardly takes thirty seconds, and I go on my way, forgetting the little girl. I slow down in front of the motley crowd waiting for the offices of the administrative center to open. The talk seems desultory, the sun is still barely visible. The flag with its bands of blue, white, and red floats on high. In front of the closed gates there's still time to have hopes of taking a numbered ticket that will entitle you to see an official, to explain your case, your life, the whys and wherefores of it all, to hand in the form requesting permission to remain, to ask for a receipt, to enquire about a temporary residence permit, to hope for a renewal, a hearing, an extension, an open sesame.

On the other pavement, more or less across the street, is the other motley crowd, the one for the clinic. A hundred tickets a day are issued there and some people have been waiting since four o'clock in the morning. Here, too, it's still calm. As I walk by, the two groups are almost touching. I'm in the middle and I wonder how many of them, either those on my right, or those on my left, arrived in *kwassa-kwassas*, those makeshift boats into which illegal immigrants coming from other Comoros Islands are crammed.

That's what I remember: weaving my way discreetly between the two groups, just as I might slip between two sharp knife blades and, once beyond them, I can't help taking a deep breath with a feeling of relief.

I keep walking right down to the landing stage: on the way I buy bananas, peppers, tomatoes. I inhale the smell of this land that I love, I peer into the depths of the water, I admire the women. I like watching the children as they come and dive into the harbor. They take off from the concrete jetty, their black legs as thin as sticks scampering nimbly along. When they reach the end they hurl themselves into the ocean, lifting their knees high and flinging their arms out wide, shouting for joy.

When the ferry, the blue-and-white vessel that makes the crossing from Petite-Terre to Grande-Terre, comes alongside, I spot Cham from a long way off, more handsome every day, more unreal every day in that he belongs to me.

We go home, we sleep, we make love, and we wake up in the middle of the day. When I'm not working, I like looking out into the night from our balcony. It's blue in some places, black in others. Hundreds of stars are massed together in the sky. I like hearing the wingbeats of the flying foxes. Out on the expanse of the sea little yellow dots move like fireflies. These are the lights on the fishermen's boats, they go out with oil lamps attached to their masts to attract the fish.

I have such a longing for this country, a longing to take it all in, gulping down the sea in long drafts, consuming the sky mouthful after mouthful.

I'm twenty-nine and you must believe me. Every day the waiting intensifies, every day buoys up the hope of having a child. For me the months slip by with dreams, laughter, and cuddles. Nursery rhymes come back to me from my childhood as if by magic. *Turn turn little mill clap clap little hands* and my head is a gourd filled with things that seem to be within reach but nevertheless elude me. There are so many children here, so many pregnant women, all these babies held in so many arms, why not in mine? All these babies born without anyone even wanting them, while I'm praying, begging. When the hot blood comes in my underwear every month I weep and curse all these mothers I see in the hospital who don't have a clue, all these illegal immigrants coming to give birth on this French island so as to get papers and I hold myself back from asking them *Did you really want this baby or did you just want to come to Mayotte and get your papers?*

I'm changing. I'm filling out, but there's nothing more on me than bad fat, my head's in a spin and my words are turning sour like milk. Every morning all the poor wretches waiting for their papers as well as the others waiting for medical treatment irritate me, there are too many of them, they're too noisy, too this, too that. You must believe me. I'm going mad, I'm no longer myself. I'm reeling.

I'm thirty and that's all I do: wait and weep.

One day at dawn, when I'm about to complete my tour of duty at the hospital, the blood comes. I'd worked it out the day before, six days late and in my head, oh in my head if you only knew what was going on in my head, I had a baby, I had a name for it, I had stories for it *Fly fly little bird swim swim little fish in the water*, I had a lovely christening, I was a *maman* in traditional Mahorian dress and all Cham's family were paying their respects to me for this mixed race baby who'd have a good djinn to watch over him all his life.

I walk carefully, I tread lightly, I say prayers, I go to the little church in Dzaoudzi and light three candles. I pray so hard that there's a buzzing in my ears. But at dawn the thick, sticky blood comes trickling between my legs and I go home, I don't pick up any packages of cookies, no apple, no orange, and when I get to the corner I see her, but I don't really see her, all I can feel is the blood between my legs and I'd like to stitch up this vulva of mine with thick black thread to stop it flowing. I walk past the little girl without a glance and hear *Hey! Hey!* I turn and she smiles at me, holding out her hands like that, empty.

You must believe me, I've turned into a madwoman. I pick up a stick and start running at her, yelling I can't remember what, maybe *Get lost*, yes maybe that's it, and it's as if I were driving away a mangy dog. She bolts away swiftly and I can't follow her up the hill amid bushes and filth. I throw the stick at her back. She yells and so do I.

I'm thirty-one and Cham has left me. He already has another woman, from one of the Comoros Islands. I don't know where he met her. The whore. She wears brightly colored clothes that I call clown costumes and a sandalwood mask which gives her the face of a clown. She's a whore of a clown. She has prominent buttocks, her skin's yellow and black. *So do you fancy a taste of black meat now? Fucking little illegal immigrants? My mother was right, you men are all the same. Nice is it, fucking blacks?* That's what I ask Cham as the thick red blood flows between my legs and his hand smacks my cheek. At that moment, you must believe me, I wished he'd hit me again and again, and drive the woman uttering such horrible things right out of me!

Sometimes at night when I'm alone in the house, I long to hear once again, the moist sound our bodies used to make sliding back and forth against one another, I long to hear the wingbeats of the flying foxes outside, and to fall asleep lulled by Cham's gentle snoring.

I long to lie watching the blades of the electric ceiling fan turn as we made love. When I'm alone and frail and lost yet again, I pretend to clasp Cham's body, inhaling his scent, licking his sweat. I'm washing away those wounding words with my tongue, I'm swallowing all my rage, I'm polishing the surface of our love with my body, so that it is smooth and silky once more.

But Cham no longer loves me, he looks at me with dull eyes and a wry grimace on his lips, and demands a divorce. I refuse him. He disappears for days on end and then tells me he's got married in a religious ceremony and I badmouth him again, but I still don't want a divorce. I've lost all reason. My rage, my frustration, my bitterness take over and no one can save me. He announces that his whore of a clown is expecting a child. I loathe this country.

I'm almost thirty-three. Sometimes I happen to pass Cham's whore pushing a stroller through the streets of Mamoudzou. She has no papers and every so often I long to denounce her the way people used to during the war. I imagine all it would take would be a phone call to the border police and then I could quietly wait outside her house and watch them kicking out the bitch, winkling her out, putting her into their jeep *Bye bye clown whore, back to Anjouan the one way ticket's free.* But the red stroller stops me because not so long ago, I too had dreamed of pushing a stroller like that through the streets of Mamoudzou. So I go on my way.

I'm almost thirty-three and that night, May 3, I'm working. It has been pouring rain for several days, there are not many people about and I'm in the nurses' room, alone, reading a book: I have no friends anymore, I no longer see the ones who knew me when I was with Cham. In any case I no longer have any inclination for things like that, moonlit evenings, endless chats about this country, poverty, and decay. These days Patrick, the nursing assistant, is the only one who still talks to me. Sometimes when I see him with his flowery shirt, his belly like a globule of oil, when I notice his roving eye lighting upon the young black women, I try to picture the Patrick who came to Mayotte fifteen years ago with a wife and children. Back then did he smell of cigarettes, sweat, and eau de cologne as he does now, had he already closed his heart and mind, did he dream of spending his Friday evenings at Ninga disco, enthroned like a nabob, surrounded by those young women from the Comoros Islands and Madagascar who perfume their vaginas with deodorant? Had he tried to resist at least or, once he'd understood the power a white man has here, did he just go with the flow? But I don't judge him, this country crushes us, this country turns us all into beings who do wrong, this country clamps its pincers around us and we can no longer get away. The telephone rings and I'm told the emergency services have just taken in the people from two medical *kwassa-kwassas*. I put down my book and take a deep breath. Those are the ones I fear the most. Those medical *kwassa-kwassas* bring in sick people, the elderly, pregnant women, disabled children, people who are badly injured or burned, or mad. They make the crossing between the island of Anjouan and Mayotte to receive treatment. I've seen women with cancers that are so far advanced that in mainland France they no longer exist outside medical textbooks. I've seen badly burned people, their skin totally rotted away, babies dead for several days but still in their mothers' arms, men with their legs bitten off by sharks.

I'm almost thirty-three, I close my book and maybe that evening I forget to close my heart. When I go down to the reception area, there are already a dozen people there, all soaked to the skin. Several heavily pregnant women, an old woman with one leg, an adolescent boy jumping up and down on the spot and clinging to one of the firemen and a very beautiful young woman with a baby in her arms. I notice her at once, she's sixteen or seventeen, she looks very healthy, her gaze is that of a frightened animal, flitting restlessly from left to right. The emergency workers escort the pregnant women toward the maternity ward and, for once, my mind's a blank. I wish them no ill. The fireman to whom the adolescent boy is clinging walks over to me, saying *He's nuts.* Then the youth starts laughing and it reminds me of Cham's laughter. Something strong, gentle, and infectious. I point out the floor for the psychiatric unit. The boy goes on laughing and his peals of laughter mingle with the sound of the rain. The fireman asks me to keep an eye on the others until the police arrive. He moves off quickly but for a long time I can still hear the boy's laughter.

Then the old woman with one leg stands up, leaning on a long stick that serves her as a crutch, and moves toward the exit. She gives me a sideways glance but I keep my hands in my coat pockets, I don't stop her, I don't assist her, I watch her hopping toward the door and disappearing into the Mamoudzou night, in the rain. She's made it, she's in France. I beckon to the young woman to approach and we go into cubicle number 2. Her baby is wrapped in a traditional red and yellow fabric. It's not crying, doesn't stir. Is it dead, maybe? Outside the rain falls with a noise like machine-gun fire.

Deftly the young woman extracts the baby from its swaddling clothes and I realize that it's been bandaged up like a mummy. Has it suffered burns? She undoes the strips that just partially cover its face. It's a baby barely a few days old, it's breathing, it's not been burned, it looks perfect. He *is* perfect. I begin to speak but the mother puts her finger to her lips and goes *Shh!* She doesn't want him to be woken up. She points to one of the baby's eyes. I don't understand, I can see nothing, the baby's asleep. She becomes impatient, she points to her two eyes, then to mine, then to those of the baby. *Oh, is your baby blind?* She shakes her head vigorously and suddenly the baby begins to wriggle, smacks its lips once or twice, as if it is searching for the nipple, and the young woman holds it out to me as you might do with something that both frightens and disgusts you. I don't know why I take this baby that's being handed to me and the infant stretches out in my arms and this warm little body snuggling up to me is wonderful. The child opens its eyes. The mother shrinks back against the bed and what I see, now, is incredible, I've never seen such a thing in my life, it's simply something I learned the correct term for during my training. The baby has one dark eye and one green one. It's affected by heterochromia, a totally benign genetic anomaly. The green of its eye is like the green of the leaves of the breadfruit tree, no, of the mango, oh, I don't know anymore, during winter in the southern hemisphere the greens of trees in this country are sometimes incredible. He looks at me with a bicolored gaze, I speak to him, saying *Hello, pretty baby*. Then the mother says to me, making wild gestures toward the little boy *Him baby of the djinn. Him bring bad luck with his eye. Him bring bad luck.* I place him gently in the crib and raise the bars and tell the mother I'm going to fetch a bottle. As I turn my back, I hear her say *You love him, you take him.* I don't pause in my tracks, I let these words pursue me like a wonderful trail of stars in the night over Mayotte. During those few minutes as I go into the nursery to prepare a bottle, my thoughts unfurl like flowers in the morning, wide open and happy; I picture myself in my house with a baby, a crib, a whole array of games, of books for reading. *The little mill turned the little hands clapped the little bird flew the little fish swam.* I'm almost thirty-three and at last I have a child.

I'm thirty-four and you must believe me when I say that I'm the *maman* of a boy called Moïse. When I came back with the bottle of milk the beautiful girl was no longer there. I remember what I did. I fed the child, I washed him, I dressed him in a stretchy onesie decorated with little gray elephants, I put him to bed in a cradle in the nursery. I put a little blue band on his wrist and I marked it M. I telephoned Cham. He picked up at the first ring and listened attentively, in silence, the way I used to listen in the old days to tales of his childhood. You must believe me. In the place where I'm speaking to you from lies are pointless. In exchange for a divorce I asked him to recognize this child, to give it his name and tell everyone he was a son he'd had with an illegal immigrant and that I, his ex-wife, had agreed to bring him up. A false certificate of paternity in exchange for a real divorce. He agreed.

Let no one presume to judge me. I took advantage of all this country's flaws, this island's flaws, all those turning a blind eye. And it was so easy, believe me. How many men impregnate women from the Comoros Islands, from Madagascar and are obliged to recognize their children? How many men are professional frauds in the business of acknowledging paternity? How many children are abandoned by their parents? How many parents disown their children on board the *kwassa-kwassas* when the border police intercept them? How many children, with no parents and no papers spend all day here playing beneath the sun without anyone ever asking them anything at all?

Let no one presume to judge me. I've known police, lawyers, judges and journalists all of whom came to this country with their great ideas and quickly, too quickly, succumbed, when confronted by the hosts of beautiful women lingering on street corners, in cafés, in discos. When Cham came to give me the certificate, I almost said to him *Look at us Cham. Look how happy we are now.*

I'm forty-four and Moïse, my son, tells me his dearest wish would be to taste snow. That is quite strange. He asks me if it's a good wish and I answer yes. I ought to tell him how I, too, loved it when the snow fell in my deep valley and when, gradually, everything became white and silent and magical. I ought to tell him how I ate great handfuls of snow, but I don't, the words remain stuck in my throat, hurting me like fishhooks. Moïse is a boy who only laughs rarely and discreetly and whose grace moves me every day. When he walks, when he runs, when he does his homework, when he plays, when he's asleep. Where does this come from, his mother or his father? Had I glimpsed it, this grace, that day when his mother offered him to me and he stretched out in my arms, so warm, so tiny? One day I must tell him about that moment, but I don't want to think about it, not right away. I want to live this life which is sweet, which I relish a sip at a time, so as not to squander it. Moïse goes to the private school in Pamandzi, where there are only French children or the children of people from Mayotte who've spent a long time in France. Occasionally someone makes a remark to him about his eye but Moïse knows how to pronounce "heterochromia" correctly. Last year he even gave a talk about it to his class. He never asks anything about his biological parents. I like telling him he was born in my heart, that I crossed continents and seas to find him and spent a long time waiting for him. That pleases him. Moïse always finishes his food, leaving nothing on his plate and I think this comes from a long way back, the truth he carries within himself and which he's not fully aware of. The truth that causes him to scrape his plate, eat an apple whole, seeds, core, and all, never make demands, make himself light, make himself invisible.

I now work during the day at the hospital but I live on Petite-Terre on the hill above Pamandzi, from where I can see the airport, the lagoon, and at night, the lights of the fishermen's boats. In our courtyard there's a frangipani tree, an ylang-ylang tree, an allamanda, a mango, a papaya, and banana palms. Not far from us there are corrugated iron huts, *bangas* where illegal immigrants live and we double-lock our house, put iron grilles over the windows and padlocks on our gate. We have a dog now. We've called him Bosco because Moïse's favorite book is *The Boy and the River* by Henri Bosco. Our Bosco is a mongrel I picked up near the hospital. He's black with ugly gray patches on his body, from a distance it looks as if he has mange, but no, they are just patches. I wondered whether he, too, had arrived on a *kwassa-kwassa*, along with his master, and a few goats and chickens. This dog hung around near the hospital for several days and in the end I adopted him. Cham lives on the island of Réunion with his wife and these days she has papers and three more children. During the summer holidays I occasionally see him but he looks away quickly and I think I've hurt him too much for him still to remember the young woman I once was and whom he married. I have no friends, I lead an isolated existence with my son that suffices. When I take the ferry home at the end of the afternoon, I gaze with fresh eyes into the depths of the water, at the women on the boat, at the little islands and the hill of Kaweni above Mamoudzou, where the shantytown spreads its tentacles like an octopus. I see the children wandering aimlessly about there, playing on the market square, and I think about those pregnant women who arrived here in the rain on the same day as Moïse and all the others who've come before or since. The maternity hospital in Mamoudzou has become the largest in France. What have they done with their children? Have they left them with a big brother, an uncle, an aunt? What will happen to the children in their teens? I don't know.

Outside a flying fox is moving to a different tree and its wingbeats remind me of another life. I smile. As I'm tidying up and Moïse is building what he says will be a whole town with his Legos, we listen to a little music, I put on some Barbara, the way my mother used to long ago. It's strange how such things jog our memories.

When "L'aigle noir," "The Black Eagle," comes on, we wait for our favorite bits of the track and sing along in chorus, me in the kitchen, him in the living room. *Hey, bird, hey, take me far away. Take me back to that land of long ago, the way it was*

in my childhood dreams, catching at stars with a trembling hand.
The way it was in my childhood dreams, the way it was on a cloud
in the sky, the way it was to light up the sun, to make the rain
fall, and make wonders unfold.

That evening we reread *The Boy and the River*, which Moïse
adores.

When we first began reading it we had an illustrated
dictionary beside us so he could see what reeds look like, or
a duck, or a shad, or a May tree. Often Moïse is the boy,
Pascalet. Sometimes he's the river. This evening he's lying
on his back, his slim body motionless, eyes half closed. His
left hand lies palm up in my lap. He's listening, knows every
sentence, every comma, he knows this book by heart. This
evening can he hear my voice shaking and lingering over the
words as I read the following passage?

What country? From where had Gatzo journeyed to
the island? Who was he?

I asked myself these questions, but never dared to
put them to him. He never asked me any. I, too, was a
mystery to him. My presence on the island, my unex-
pected appearance must have puzzled him. But he
showed no curiosity about these miraculous happenings
which only I seemed to find wonderful.

For there were moments when I told myself that I
was living in a dream, a terrifying yet delicious dream . . .

How, if it were not a dream, could I have found
myself, after so many adventures, alone with a boy

whose name was the only thing I knew of him, and on this boat, this hidden boat, lost from human sight among the reeds up a backwater which led nowhere?

Here's what I remember. Moïse had fallen asleep. I'm gazing at him and suddenly this extraordinary notion occurs to me that he looks like me. Yes, there, just where the glow from the nightlight rests on him, something in the fall of the eyelid, the arch of the eyebrow, the beginnings of the nose. I go up to him and I say to him *Good night my son.*

I'm forty-six and I'm trying to write a letter but I can't manage it. I'm leaning forward, the upper part of my body almost lying across the paper, as if I were hoping that not just my hand but the whole of my body might be forming the words. Things are not well with Moïse. He has nightmares and he's full of anger. He no longer wants to go to school and sometimes I come across him in the corrugated iron shelter by the landing stage in Dzaoudzi, waiting for me to come home from work. I need to tell him about that night, that night when the whole island was awash with rain, that blessed day when he came to me. I can't bring myself to tell him to his face, I look at him and the words stick in my throat. But I can't bring myself to write it either. The night, the rain, the medical *kwassa-kwassa* that had landed on the beach down at Bandrakouni in the south, the swaddled baby. How can I tell him all that?

I'm forty-seven and I remember having a persistent headache. I know I ought to go and see a doctor but I don't do it.

I'm in pain and I tell myself I deserve it. Moïse comes home late and when I hear Bosco making the noise he keeps only for him, something between a bark and a human cry, my shoulders finally relax, I can breathe a little. Sometimes I think about that house where I lived as a child, long since empty, and the absurd thought occurs to me that back there now I'd be alright. I'd escape from the heat drilling into my head, I'd escape from this country that I sometimes feel is boiling over with rage. I'd take Moïse far away from here. I finally plucked up the courage to talk to him. To tell him his story. I began like this *It was May 3, it was raining, your mother arrived in a* kwassa-kwassa *on the beach at Bandrakouni.* I thought all that would be enough for him but no, every day he wants me to talk about it again, to tell it over and over, to tell it more slowly, to remember colors, shapes, precise words, but I have such a bad headache that I no longer want to go back over the same thing and Moïse loses his temper, he calls me a liar, he wants to go and visit the beach at Bandrakouni, but how can I tell him that it's only a beach, there's nothing waiting for him there. Moïse, my son, no longer calls me Mam, he calls me Marie. He says I've brought him up as a white, I've kept him from living out his "real life," and this was not what he was destined for. He plays hooky from school, he hangs around, he asks for money all the time, he resents me. I can see it in his green eye.

I'm forty-seven and I'm listening at his door, he's asleep. I knock *It's time to get up, Moïse. You'll be late for school.*

I think about that house in the valley. It's cold back there. I should be wearing a warm robe and thick socks. The deep, unbroken, mellow silence of the white mountains would reign there. What do we know of our hearts and of the things of our childhood that grab us by the ankle and suddenly bring us up with a jolt. I think about the baby with the green eye and the way his mother, that young woman, who seemed like a child herself, had swaddled him. What do I know of Moïse's heart? What do I know of the invisible and powerful things that grab him by the ankle?

I hear him waking up, maybe today he'll go to school, and won't wear that cap that covers half his face, maybe today he won't hang around with that scruffy boy he met some time ago, maybe today he'll bear his green eye proudly aloft, the way one bears a good luck charm? Maybe today he'll call me "Mam" again? I put out his favorite bowl on the counter in the kitchen, the one with his name on, the pain's like a white hot dagger boring into my head. I open the sealed container where I keep the cereals. I hear Moïse coming along the corridor and outside the window, all of a sudden, I see my mother. She's standing there, looking in at me with profoundly sad eyes. I understand at once.

You must believe me. In the place where I'm speaking to you from lies are pointless. I didn't feel the artery bursting in my brain, I didn't feel the last spasm of my heart. You must believe me when I say that I felt no pain when my head struck the ground and my arm became twisted under my body at a strange angle. You must believe me when I say that I stayed standing beside myself and that the worst is yet to come.

Moïse

It's a big cell. It's square. A concrete bench runs along the wall facing the door.

On the same wall, high up, there's a rectangular opening that might possibly let a cat through. Or a very thin dog, like Bosco.

I'm sitting on the bench. If I look up I can see a fragment of sky that's so blue and motionless that I wonder if it's not a picture. There's a word for them, those things, pictures painted to look like the real thing, I can't remember it now, if Marie were here she'd have . . .

My hands are starting to shake, I shouldn't have thought about Marie. I try to steady them between my thighs, to squeeze them under my armpits, to cross my fingers as if I were praying with all my strength but it doesn't stop.

My name's Moïse, I'm fifteen years old and at dawn I killed someone. I'd like them to know I barely squeezed the trigger, if Marie were here I'd have told her that, I'd have told her like this *I barely squeezed it Mam and it went off*, and she'd have believed me, but it's more than a year now that Marie's been gone. I'm alone and I killed Bruce in the woods at dawn. Bruce with his barbarian's heart and his sick brain and his serpent's tongue. Bruce, who did that to me . . .

I killed him.

He crumpled up and an *uh* emerged from his throat like a choking gasp and after that, there in the woods, for long minutes there was nothing but the day dawning and that pink glow slicing through the branches, bearing down on Bruce like knife blades. The pistol was hot, hard, and heavy in my hand. I gripped it firmly and felt its energy mounting up my arm like thousands of burning needles.

I sat down on the ground. Between Bruce and me there was a carpet of dry eucalyptus leaves. I pictured him standing there beside his own body, half-dead, half-alive, the way he used to stand when he'd been smoking spice, his head tilted on one side, his hands in his hair, his fingers twisting his frizzy curls rapidly this way and that, unable to stop this nervous tic, wondering what the hell he's doing here, stretched out among the eucalyptus trees with that stain on his T-shirt. Can he see me, this half-dead, half-alive Bruce? Is he starting to forget who he is or, on the contrary, is everything clear, everything plain? Does he see his whole life spread out before him, does he have regrets, or is he as filled with rage as ever?

This island turned us into dogs, Bruce. You, who'd chosen the nickname of a superhero, Bruce Wayne, you once explained to me, while jumping up and down on the spot as if you had springs in your feet. Bruce Wayne, Batman, because you liked bats, or at least that's what you told me, although for my part, I never saw you liking anything other than smoking spliffs and dominating other people.

This island has made me into a killer. Do you remember

how you used to say to me *No Mercy Mo*, well you see, Bruce, this morning I had none for you.

I slipped the gun back into my rucksack, and thought about everything it contained from my past life, from that life when I lived in a house built from rectangular, pinkish bricks, when the nighttime was for dogs, flying foxes, and thieves and I was not yet a dog, a thief, a killer but just a boy with one green eye and one dark eye. I thought about how this black, weighty gun was now lying there next to my book and Marie's scarf, I pictured the black pistol possibly getting caught up with her identity card, maybe the barrel of the murder weapon was pointing at the photo of Marie in the top right-hand corner of her card. I told myself that if I stuck my head into the rucksack now, the way I like to do, because I imagine that things from the past have a smell of their own and that this smell, unlike people and dogs, lasts for ever, well, you see, sometimes it's only this fantasy of a smell that lasts for ever that keeps me from going mad, yes, I told myself that if I stuck my head into my bag now, there'd be nothing but gunpowder, iron and blood and that, there you are, such was my life now.

I stood up and left Bruce in the woods. I walked and walked, I kept my head down, I didn't look at the early-morning streets, I didn't look at the sky, I didn't look at the sea, I walked all the way here, I waited by the gate and the cop opened it to me. I said *I've killed a boy up there in the woods near Lake Dziani. The pistol's in my rucksack* and the cop looked at me like he'd seen a ghost. At the desk I gave them precise directions and they put me in here. In this cell.

The edges of the bench are rough and graze the back of my knees. These little abrasions are nothing much, but for me, who's known nights in the open, bare-fisted fights, chases through the woods, the fire of a knife across my face, my toes nibbled by rats, hunger, solitude, fear, real fear I mean, the kind that makes you shit yourself, for me today, having just killed a human being, these little abrasions are unbearable.

I shift in the hope of finding a place where the edge of the bench is smooth but no, it's like that all the way along. It's as if all the people who've been here before me had picked away at this concrete bench with their fingernails. Fingernails bursting with rage and despair.

I get up and go to sit on the ground. Maybe it's all passed out of me now, the despair, the fury, the violence, the feelings that gnaw at you from inside and drive you to pick away at a concrete bench, aim great kicks at the door, kill, or bang your head against the wall like that guy was doing who was here earlier.

He was here when I came in. He said nothing, he simply moved along to the end of the bench, keeping his head down. His pants made a little scraping sound against the concrete. He smelled of grass, of earth, of rain and wind, as if he were nature itself. It was very strange. As for me, I hadn't washed for I don't know how many days and I'd killed someone that morning. Do you have a particular smell when you become a killer? I stopped looking at him, in any case there'd be no point in sussing him out, noticing what he wore, or how he wore it, the shape of his head or anything else. I didn't greet him, I didn't ask him why are you here. What point would there be in knowing where he was from, what his name was or that kind of thing. Maybe it's better like that, no more speaking, no more seeing, no more knowing.

Hardly had I sat down and felt the first bite from the bench when that guy stood up. He began moving forward slowly, really slowly, he took a small step, sliding one flip-flop along the ground and bringing the other one up beside it, waited for I don't know what, then began again with another little sliding step and stopped again. I watched his strange maneuvers with fascination. Was he crazy? Was he having visions like the ones I'd been having during these past few weeks? When he got to the end, he arranged his flip-flops carefully so that they were neatly lined up side by side and all at once began banging his head against the wall with incredible speed. *Boom boom boom.* Stupidly, it took me several seconds to react, I wasn't expecting that guy to do such a thing, and for a moment, I thought I didn't want to have anything to do with that kind of misery, yet all the same I stood up and pulled the man backward while calling out for help.

He fell back limply into my arms without struggling, like a dead bird, as if that was all he'd been waiting for. His clothes were soft and of good quality and that whole earth smell of his filled my head completely. Two policemen came in and took him away, saying *Monsieur! Monsieur! Wake up, Monsieur!*

Bolts groaned, latches clicked, keys turned. A moment later a vehicle drove off outside. Soon he'd be in the hospital. In

27

the firm, knowledgeable hands of doctors, with the soothing words of a nurse who'd come to see him at regular intervals, in that clean, odorless linen he'd have to wear, his head would be x-rayed, the white sheets on which he'd lie down, the painkillers, the antidepressants, the antidotes to death, the sleep into which he'd fall heavily with arms outstretched. A sweet respite which would last for several days until he returned here: to this cell.

The cop from this morning comes back, without my rucksack.

"You all right?"

I don't reply.

"You hungry?"

I think about the ones outside with empty bellies, roaming around the houses, the grilled meat stalls, driven nuts by the blue scent of roasting chicken, I think about the ones hiding behind restaurants and bakeries, it's only yesterday that I was one of them.

"Can I have my bag back?!"

"Not yet. Don't you want anything to eat?"

"No. I just want my rucksack."

"OK. Soon."

His voice is gentle and serious, the voice of an adult who knows things, one who could understand everything, fix things. Suddenly I want to cry. I wonder if he's opened my book, if he's read my name on the back of the cover, if he's noticed the pages where the corners are turned down, if the pages that are coming loose from wear and tear have caught his eye. I'd like to tell him that I'm not just a killer, I was once a boy who read books, who listened to music, who was an ace at Legos, I'd like to tell him that I didn't know how to fight back against Bruce, that I've been cowardly and stupid, that for months I was paralyzed by fear. I'd like to tell him that all this, this filthy body, these rags that serve me as clothes, this hand that held the gun . . .

I suddenly hear Bruce's *Uh.* The sound comes from just here, beside me. I look around but there's nothing there. I close my eyes and say:

"I barely squeezed it this morning. The gun just went off."

"You didn't mean to kill him? It was an accident?"

I see Bruce emerging from between the eucalyptus trees like an apparition of the devil, I didn't stop to wonder how he'd found me, I pulled out the pistol and that's when he called me *Mo, my darlin'* with that smile that I want to wipe off his face because I know what's in his mind, I remember how he, what he did to me . . .

"Tell me. Was it an accident?"

"No, I wanted to kill him."

My own words are swirling around me like large birds with giant wings and nothing in my life has ever been as true as this.

"Ah. You'll be brought before the magistrate this afternoon or tomorrow."

"My bag."

"Don't think about that now. Get some rest, Moïse."

This use of my name gives me a shock and my hands begin

shaking again. The cop goes off but I know he's still standing outside the door he's just bolted.

No one's called me Moïse for a long time. Out there among all the wild boys like me, who dream of their *mamans* in their sleep at night, I'm Scarface Mo. Yes, as they say Mo, they make a swift gesture like this, starting at the right eyebrow and ending on the cheek. Behind my back they say I'm the child of a djinn and that I've gone nuts. Some of them think Mo is for Mohammed, but the only time I've ever set foot in a mosque was to steal a piece of carpet or some slippers or to eat there at night during Ramadan or Eid.

I miss my bag and, in spite of myself, my hands pat the ground, feeling for the shape of it. That dark brown rucksack used to belong to Marie. She took it with her when she went to work, carrying it over one shoulder. It's made of a kind of synthetic fabric that's resistant to everything; to mud, rain and even the Mayotte sun that can crack open concrete paving stones and make asphalt explode. Every night I rest my head on it like a pillow. Inside this rucksack are my book, *The Boy and the River*, Marie's French identity card, a knife I found yesterday in Stéphane's kitchen, and a scarf with a blue and green pattern that belonged to Marie. She liked to wear it around her neck on evenings when we went out to eat chicken and coconut at Nassuf's. On those occasions she left the brown rucksack at home and took a canvas shoulder bag embroidered with threads of gold and bright blue. For how much longer will I carry memories of that bag, the way the threads were woven to create a symbol in the shape of a drop of water?

Last night I had a dream about the house. I was hiding on the old children's playground at the beginning of Moya Road. Well screened from view by big mango trees, it's an area that can't be seen from the road but I had a clear memory of it. The earth is all uneven and cracked. When it rains the ground becomes an expanse of red mud and days go by before all the water evaporates. The only fruits produced by those mango trees are bitter and fibrous, it only takes a few mouthfuls to give you stomach cramps and violent diarrhea. In summer the mangoes fall and slowly rot. The mosquitoes and midges lay their eggs on them. At night they're nibbled by squeaking rats. When the sun is high in the sky, lean stray dogs come to sleep there in the shade of the dense foliage. On this playground there's a concrete ping-pong table. You can still see the line marked for the net. I've never seen a soul on Mayotte playing ping-pong, but, as Marie used to say, just because you've never seen it that doesn't mean it doesn't exist. This table seemed to me a good place to sleep: high up on the cool smooth surface, safe from the rodents and the dogs. I rested my head on my rucksack and stretched out there. The night was silent, dense and hot. It bore down on me and it felt as though it might swallow me, painlessly and gently.

I took out the knife and made several figures in the air, as if I could slice the night into pieces and cram these pieces into my mouth. I remembered those evenings at the house when Marie used to play her record of Barbara. In those days the night stayed outside, the night was for dogs, flying foxes, thieves. I formed the words with the tips of my lips. *Hey, bird, hey, take me far away. Take me back to that land of long ago, the way it was in my childhood dreams, catching at stars with a trembling hand. The way it was in my childhood dreams, the way it was on a cloud in the sky, the way it was to light up the sun, to make the rain fall, and make wonders unfold.* Then I'd go back to the beginning, again and again, until sleep overcame me.

I dreamed I was back at the house. I had the body of a child again, warm, flexible, soft. There was no scar on my face. There was music playing and slanted rays of sunlight poured into the living room, making patterns on the tiled floor. It was clean, it smelled good. I was playing, running from one room to another, jumping from one patch of light to another, from one patch of warmth to another.

I wonder why a part of me refuses to accept that it's all over, all that time *at the house,* the solid concrete walls, the colored curtains at the windows, the filmy mosquito nets, the green corrugated iron roof on which the rain danced like a peashooter, the mango tree with its sweet fruits in the yard, the scent of the ylang-ylang as dusk fell, hot meals, *The Boy and the River,* school, games, homework, showers and *Le Petit Marseillais* soap, white cotton shirts, squares of chocolate, the letter "X" in Scrabble, *petit beurre* cookies, "L'aigle noir," nights of deep sleep, days with thoughts of nothing other than play. Where is this unbreakable thing hidden? Is it in that mysterious place known as the unconscious, that word which Marie taught me when she talked about the past? This is what she said, Marie, and this is how she said it, her hands joined together in prayer. *You may have forgotten but it's in your hidden memory, my love. The unconscious never forgets.*

I stretch out on the cool floor of the cell that reminds me of the ping-pong table. Maybe I sleep a little, maybe I dream of the dense, endless night that can be sliced into pieces and swallowed. Maybe I'm still singing, *Hey, bird, hey, take me far away . . .*

Bruce

Uh.

Behind Mo there's a weeping woman. I say *Hey, behind you* but Mo does nothing, he's staring at the ground at my feet. He still has that frigging gun in his hands. I don't know where he got it from, must be his pal Stéphane who gave him the thing. If it turned out to be only a toy, that wouldn't surprise me with Mo, he's such a coward. I look at the woman who's still weeping and tell her *Get lost!* But she doesn't move, it's as if she can't hear me. Who is she, anyway? Mo has a knack of attracting all the *muzungus*, it must be the way he talks good French with all that *Monsieur Madame s'il vous plaît*. Fuck off, Mo.

I came here to settle accounts with you. I've got a knife in my pocket and know what needs to be done. *Come here, my darlin'*. I'm not scared of you and your toy gun, you think you can play the hard man but don't have a clue. Yesterday you humiliated me in front of everyone, how the fuck could you do that to me, you know I'm the one has to win in the ring, I win all *mourengué* fights, I'm the strongest, the king of Gaza.

Then you snuck away like a thief but I knew you'd come here. I've been waiting for you since last night Mo. Do you remember how you told me about this place, and how your mother, you know the one you called your mother, the *muzungu* who dropped down dead without anyone hitting her, without anyone scaring her, a typical whitey's death, a death for rich people whose trash cans are full to overflowing? So there's this *bweni*, this female, standing there in her kitchen putting cereal into your bowl for you and you hear a noise *crash bang wallop* and she's dead. And she used to bring you here, this woman you told me all about it, using your good little boy's words, the good boy who'd been to school, and you told me it was your favorite place and believe me that day I almost went for you and tore you apart like a papaya, every frigging bit of you, your green eye, your blood, your shirt, your mouth, your fucking rucksack, your balls, your prick, your heart, I wanted to see all that on the ground, on my hands and on the walls.

I suppose you think I was born like this, and all I ever wanted to do was hit and bite and beat people up, but me too, I'd've liked it if I could talk in a little voice with a faraway look in my eyes about my favorite place here in this country. Me too, I'd've liked someone to fix me a bowl of cereal, fucking cereal, I don't even know what cereal tastes like, d'you think I wouldn't have liked someone to take me for a picnic by Lake Dziani or on its island of sand, or go swimming with the dolphins? To go see my own country, d'you think I wouldn't have liked that, too? I should've kicked you out of Gaza the very first day, that's what dropped me in the shit. La Teigne warned me, said having you around wasn't good for business. He told me you were a nutjob and in the end it'd all go fuckries.

I should've listened to that dumb bastard. OK let's be done with it. Come here Mo, I don't want to hang around here on Petite-Terre any longer. La Teigne and Rico are down by the ferry already, they're waiting for me.

You don't speak. Why are you looking down at the ground like that and why's she bawling? What's on the ground that's so interesting . . . ?

Shit.

What's wrong, I don't get it. What've you done, Mo, tell me it's magic, tell me it's a trick you learned because you seriously are the child of the djinn, you really do have powers and that green eye of yours is still working, tell me Mo, come on, I won't hurt you. I'm putting my knife away, I don't have a knife anymore, look, my hands are empty. Answer me!

Mo doesn't answer. He sits on the ground and goes on looking down at my feet, just there where there's a body and it's my body but it's red and it can't be mine because I like to move around, I don't like staying like that with my eyes open, yellow eyes, I don't like it, I have to wake up.

I'm trying to get back into my body, I lean over sharpish, I want to jump back into my own body, just like that, like jumping into a puddle and get splashed all over with myself, that's mine, that body, that's me there on the ground, and every time I think I've almost got back in, out again I pop as quick as if I'd been sucked out by an outside force. I'm trying to run, to escape and I'm heading through the woods, I'm crossing the lake, but after a bit there's always this force that pulls me back here, there, at Bruce's feet. No: my feet, because *Bruce is me.*

I know nothing no more.

What am I doing there on the ground, like that, like I'm dead? Why does that woman behind you suddenly look at me?

You'll pay for this, Scarface Mo, hear me? You're dead meat but I can't get close to you, it's like there's an elastic in my back that pings me back here, to this dead body that still pisses blood.

Was it you that shot me, Mo? It makes me want to laugh, I didn't know a corpse could laugh. Don't think I'm a fool. Kids like me end up snuffing it sooner than the rest, that much I know. But if someone had told me on the day when I first saw you by the ferry, if someone had told me I'd be killed by a loser like you I'd've burst out laughing. Hey, can you hear me or what?

Mo doesn't hear. He puts the pistol away in his bag and gets up. The weeping woman looks at me for a second then she follows him. I look down at the ground and suddenly I don't give a fuck if I'm dead or alive.

Olivier

I can hear him speaking softly, I press my ear to the door but I can't tell what he's saying, it sounds like he's singing.

I can't stay here forever. There's nothing I can do for him.

I've killed a boy up there in the woods, near Lake Dziani. The pistol's in my rucksack.

That's what he said to me at the gate this morning in perfect French. It was barely seven o'clock, it was already hot and he was clutching his bag to his chest and shaking. I looked at his long scar. My right cheek began twitching but apart from that I felt nothing. I felt no surprise, it was as if I'd already lived through this moment in another life and knew that one day or another the same thing would happen to me again.

I just thought *so now it's here.*

I wanted to go and see for myself first. I didn't want instant panic. I told two of my colleagues to put the young man in with the other guy, the one who had neither his wits nor his papers but whom the border police didn't want to hold on to because he was "too unstable." They didn't want to keep him at the Dzaoudzi hospital either, the doctor on duty said to me *This isn't a mental health hospital, though if he harms himself bring him back.* That was at one o'clock in the morning. I had no choice but to keep him.

I phoned the emergency services and by chance I got through to Bacar, who, like me, prefers to work nights, at a time when you can take a break from thinking and settle down to remembering. He quickly came to pick me up in a first aid vehicle.

I was relieved to see that Misba's shop at the bottom of the slope that leads to the lake was closed. I didn't want a lot of talk and crowds gathering. We climbed rapidly up the crumbling earth slope, puffing like the two men close to retirement that we are. When we got to the top I was surprised that there was no sign of the attractive traditional building and the big explanatory notice board greeting walkers, with a breathtaking view across the lake. All that was left in its place were four iron hooks in the ground.

"What happened to the shelter?"

"It's been taken apart by illegal immigrants. You'll find bits of it here and there in their huts."

Before, we'd've exchanged jokes about how illegals pinch everything they find, a bit of wood lying around, a loose piece of paving, the landslide of stones at the foot of a slope after rain, your old underpants, your neighbor's husband.

That morning we didn't talk much.

"Do you know where to find him?"

The boy had given me such detailed instructions that you'd have thought he'd lived there all his life.

"Yes."

The lake seemed greener than usual; it felt as though we were intruders in a sanctuary. Our boots made too much noise, stirred up too much dust, the light blinded me, the wind whistled in my ears. But I moved ahead noiselessly for I knew it was only my imagination, and that from now on everything would seem more intense, more painful, more desperate, heavier, noisier.

We found him easily, and for a moment Bacar and I remained standing beside him in silence. He had new sneakers on his feet, khaki bermuda shorts, and his T-shirt was black with dried blood. His eyes, open wide, gazed up at the sky. He was just a boy.

We couldn't drag him, and had to call the chief constable who'd call the prefect. Reinforcements were needed. I could already see the headlines in the newspapers: FIRST GUN MURDER ON MAYOTTE.

I looked at the blue sky. Through the scattering of tree trunks I could see the deep green of the lake. Around us there were breadfruit trees, eucalyptus, mangoes, coconut palms. The soil was a mixture of sand and laterite. The locals say a powerful djinn lives here. I wondered if it was there beside us, trying to tell us something? Had it been there that morning at dawn when the shot was fired?

Bacar was staring at the dead boy's face. I couldn't tell if he was afraid, felt ill or was sad. Suddenly he said:

"It's Bruce."

"Bruce? Who's Bruce?"

"He's the big gang leader in Gaza."

"Shit."

The wind whistled in the branches and we looked at one another.

I don't know who it was who gave that nickname to Kaweni, the run-down neighborhood on the outskirts of Mamoudzou, but it hit the nail on the head. Gaza is a shantytown, a ghetto, a trash pile, a bottomless pit, a favela, a vast encampment of illegal immigrants, open to the skies. It's a vast steaming garbage dump that can be seen from a long way off. Gaza is a violent no-man's land where gangs of kids high on drugs make the law. Gaza is Capetown, it's Calcutta, it's Rio. Gaza is Mayotte, Gaza is France.

I closed my eyes. Maybe I was hoping it would all turn out to be a bad dream. I thought *That's done it! There's going to be war on Mayotte.*

It's been brewing for a long time, this violence, this wave of destruction, this blazing energy surging up from who knows where. Today all the dead people in the lagoon will rise up and yell in our faces and drive us mad. For a long time people have been predicting war, been on the alert for the sound of gunfire and the cries of wild animals. For a long time there have been articles, stories in the press, in-depth investigations, special assignments, visits, petitions, pamphlets, laws passed, campaigns, strikes, demonstrations, riots, promises. For a long time . . .

It's the butterfly effect exploding right in our faces.

Sometimes, after an article has appeared in a French tabloid, or after a presidential visit received lots of media coverage, I've hoped that something would happen. That someone, some-where in the teams of top civil servants who follow in the wave of ministerial visits, among the historians and intellectuals who read newspapers, that someone would truly understand what's going on here and find a solution. I'm not a historian, I'm not a politician, I'm not an intellectual, I'm not a prophet, I'm only a cop, and if I knew how to heal this country I'd say it loud and clear.

When that Syrian boy was found washed up on a Turkish beach, it gave me hope. I told myself that someone somewhere would remember this French island and would point out that here, too, children are dying on beaches. I'm only a cop, but I've seen the foam washing over their little bodies and picked up some of them like this, gently in my arms. Sometimes when I hear that a *kwassa-kwassa* has sunk in the bay, I feel a weight in my arms, as if those little bodies had never left me.

But nothing ever changes and sometimes I feel as though I'm living in a parallel dimension in which what happens here never crosses the ocean and doesn't have any effect on people. We're alone. Seen from on high and a long way off, it's true that what's here is just a handful of dust, but this dust exists, it's something real. Something that has its right side and wrong side, its sunlight and shade, its truth and lies. Lives on this land matter just as much as all those lives on other lands, don't they?

But in the end maybe it's just the same old story, one heard a hundred times before, one told a hundred times before. The story of a country that shines brightly, where everyone wants to be. There are names for it: El Dorado, mirage, paradise, chimera, utopia, Lampedusa. It's the story of those boats that people here call *kwassa-kwassas*, elsewhere they're known as barques, dugout canoes, ships, vessels. They have existed since the dawn of time, carrying people from place to place, willingly or against their will. It's the story of the human beings aboard these vessels and since the dawn of time these are the names they've been given: slaves, volunteers, lepers, convicts, repatriated settlers, Jews, boat people, refugees, stowaways, illegal immigrants.

But what am I talking about? Me, I'm just a cop who enforces the laws of France on a forgotten island. Standing in front of his body, Bruce, gang leader of Gaza, tyrant, thief, villain, I kept my eyes shut and prayed.

Marie

In the old days, to keep calm, I liked to count things. Anything, the number of people on the ferry, the taxis waiting, the coconut palms on boulevard des Crabes. With my thumbnail, I'd touch the three inner rings of each finger. Little finger one-two-three, ring finger four-five-six, middle finger seven-eight-nine, index finger ten-eleven-twelve. If need be, I'd go back to the little finger thirteen-fourteen-fifteen.

I remember it, that endless unobtrusive ballet inside my hand, and the feeling of reassurance it brought me. I miss it because I can no longer do it. I can see him, that boy Moïse has killed, he's trying to do something with his hair but it doesn't work. In the place where I'm speaking to you from we think we have fingers, hands, arms, a body, but that's not how it is at all, what subsists is like a picture, a memory of ourselves.

I'm watching Moïse on the cell floor. He's asleep and dreaming of a volcanic island. The whole island is covered in ash and amid all this grayness only one corrugated iron hut has been spared. In the place of windows and doors there are broad strips of colored fabric with geometric patterns. Blue-and-white for the three windows, purple-and-white for the door. The motifs are spots and triangles. Beside the hut is a tree with leaves as green as Moïse's eye. A baby is crying and its mother calls out. The woman can't be seen, but I know her, she's the one who offered me her child.

Moïse wakes up and looks straight at me. At first, when he did that, it gave me a start. I'd try to send him a sign, knock something over, come up close to him, but now I stay where I am, and do nothing. There's nothing to be done.

Moïse goes back to sleep. Again he's dreaming. He's in his bed, he's three or four years old and his leg is caught in the mosquito net. He's trying to disentangle himself but the mosquito net takes on a life of its own, like a white frothy snake. It climbs up his thigh, squeezes his waist, slips along his back, between his shoulder blades, grips his neck, slithers up the back of his neck, his head, appears on his forehead, slides down onto his green eye. Moïse is petrified, he cries out and in his dream I appear, I take him in my arms and say *It's all over, sweetheart, it was just a nasty bad dream.*

Me, I now know that it wasn't just a nasty bad dream but a recurrence of what he'd felt when his mother swaddled him tightly like a mummy.

Sometimes when he's asleep like this I go over to him and whisper in his ear. I tell him how much I love him, how brave he is and how sad I am at having abandoned him. I say to myself that maybe my dead woman's words will mingle with the mists of his dreams and that by and by, when he really does wake up, maybe he'll remember them.

Moïse

I used to think that on the day when I discovered the truth about my birth, something in my head would click into place. I'd shake, my mind would start racing, and all my ideas would come together, like a great jigsaw finally completed, and that suddenly I'd become an ace in my own right. And from that day on nobody would get the better of me. I'd know precisely who I was, what I was worth and what I was capable of.

Total bullshit.

When I learned the truth I felt I was less than nothing, a piece of shit, a kid that terrified its own mother when he emerged from her, a kid she handed over to the first person who came along, what do you call that? I was furious with Marie, I felt she was hiding something from me and made her repeat it over and over and over again.

It was May 3, it was raining, your mother arrived in a kwassa-kwassa *on the beach at Bandrakouni.* That'd be how she'd start telling it each evening and I was on the lookout for any mistake, sometimes she said *kwassa-kwassa*, sometimes just *kwassa* and that would make me angry, I don't know why. She refused to take me to the beach, which is at the southern end of Grande-Terre and I couldn't understand her refusal.

Maybe I accused her of being a liar, or a child thief. Maybe.

Around then, I met La Teigne who used to hang around near school on Fridays because he hoped that Moussa who was in my class and who was his "cousin" might slip him some cash. Moussa and I were friends, even if we didn't talk much. He didn't make comments about my green eye, he didn't ask me why my mother was white, he didn't ask me if I was an adopted African. Moussa liked the local music, *mgodro*, which he listened to on an old cassette player that made a jumbled noise and that I pretended to appreciate. What I liked best of all was when Moussa stood up and began dancing, his knees bent, his bottom sticking way out behind him. He pranced around like that with jerky movements. Every time the rhythm of the music changed his eyes opened wide like he was in a trance, then he burst out laughing. Moussa's parents had studied economics at Poitiers in France and it was agreed that, after Moussa had passed his *baccalauréat*, he'd do the same thing, in Poitiers. His home was just like mine. We drank Oasis and ate soft bread rolls spread with Nutella. On Fridays La Teigne often came and waited under a breadfruit tree down below the road that led to school. He seemed to camouflage himself in the shadows like a lizard. As we walked past the tree he'd suddenly appear. La Teigne spoke in a mixture of basic French and Shimaore. Moussa would give him one or two euros, if he had nothing on him he'd turn to me and I'd delve into my pockets. La Teigne would then walk away without looking back, his head held high, his shoulders thrust back. Moussa told me La Teigne, whose real name was Mahmad, was a distant cousin. Moussa's parents didn't like him spending time with La Teigne because he was an illegal immigrant. They were afraid the police might discover their distant relationship and insist on them taking him in. *We've got loads of cousins and aunts and uncles like that on Mayotte, especially on Grande-Terre. They come from Anjouan or Grande Comore and my parents say that if you give anything to just one of them, you'll end up having to feed a whole village.*

This label *illegal immigrant* wasn't something I could ignore. If Marie hadn't taken me in isn't that what I'd have been? Yet another La Teigne, dressed in shorts with dirty feet in old flip-flops and the same T-shirt for weeks at a time. Yet another La Teigne hanging around, begging. As the weeks went by it was me who gave him coins and even a note when I had one; I paid for him to have a burger, fries, and a Coke at Maoré Burger; we went to watch the planes taking off at Pamandzi. Moussa stopped going with us, on some pretext or other. I liked being with La Teigne, this thin boy who smelled of sweat and iron, and said almost nothing and walked about all day from dawn to dusk. His feet were thick, broad, with huge toenails. At night he went back on the ferry and slept in the open. He'd never been to school. When he wanted to wash he dived off the jetty at Mamoudzou. When he wanted to eat he went and picked fruit. He fascinated me, I saw him as my brother, my cousin, and pictured us as children running wild, eating wild fruits, bathing in rivers. When we went our separate ways at Dzaoudzi it seemed to me that he was going off into Life, Real Life, and I was going back to a house of lies where I was forever acting out a role in a play Marie had scripted for us.

Me: Hello.

Marie: Hello, sweetheart. Have you had a good day?

Me: Yes. I met an illegal immigrant today.

Marie: It's terrible, this business of illegal immigrants. What about some supper? We've got pasta and ham.

I didn't want any more of this sheltered life, a white person's life, white people's clothes, white music that doesn't transport you and books with their talk of reeds and willows. I wanted to sweat a black man's sweat, I wanted to eat chili pepper and cassava the way I used to eat *petit beurre* cookies and jam, I wanted drumming and yelling, I didn't want to be a *muzungu*, a foreigner. I wanted to belong somewhere, to know my real parents, to have cousins, aunts and uncles. I wanted to speak a language where the *r*'s are rolled and the *s*'s are hissed.

When I think back to that now, it makes me want to bang my head against the wall *boom boom boom*, like that guy who smelled of earth.

How long would it have lasted, that crisis? Several days or weeks? After I'd crossed the strait on the ferry, after La Teigne had revealed his true face to me, after I'd seen the shitty reality of Real Life, after I'd sweated enough, after I'd eaten and shat enough chili, I'd've quietly gone back to my solidly built house, my white person's house.

But one morning Marie collapsed *crash* on the kitchen floor. I didn't cry out, I didn't weep, I crouched down beside her. I noticed her ear was bleeding. Her eyes were wide open, as if she'd seen a ghost just before she fell, which gave her

49

face a different look. Inside my head my thoughts were racing this way and that, each of them telling me to do something: put the cereal packet away in the container so the ants can't get at it; put the milk in the fridge otherwise it'll go off; stick the pieces of the broken bowl back together; clean the counter; wake Marie; go to school; eat something before going to school; check the windows are properly closed, double-lock the door, put the latch down properly, give Bosco some food and leave water for him, press the padlock tight firmly until you hear the little *click*, shake the chain to test that it's secure, you must go now, it's time.

Outside there were all the sounds of the morning, children chatting as they set off for school, taxis honking, the neighbor sliding back his gate. I thought that if I didn't go out too, if I didn't present myself outside, to the day, to the morning, life would continue without me and I'd be stuck there like that, crouching beside Marie's body, for the rest of my life.

So I went to school, I don't know what I did there, who I spoke to, I didn't go home for lunch, I went to watch the planes taking off from the airport and I didn't stop walking until my footsteps brought me back to the house. At that moment the woman next door came out and told me Bosco had been barking without stopping since the morning. Her neck and face were red and as she said the word "barking" she put her hands over her ears. I shrugged and quickly went into the yard. Bosco came up to me, rubbing himself against my calves, thrusting his head between my legs. He kept uttering plaintive sounds *eee-eee-eee*, and I began to cry.

I don't know why I didn't call the police, the hospital, or Moussa or even the woman next door. I was fourteen, I was alone, I was afraid and, even if all those reasons aren't enough, they're all I've got.

During the night the smell grew stronger, maybe intensified by the darkness or by ghosts, I don't know. There were noises coming from the kitchen, scratching, rustling and squeaking noises. I shut myself in my room with the dog. Bosco quickly went and hid under the bed, I could hear him breathing and at intervals he came out of his hiding place, went over to the door and began growling, showing his teeth. Those were strange hours when everything seemed to be caving in all around me, I no longer knew who I really was, I no longer knew where reality ended and the nightmare began in which Marie was dead and I was alone in the world.

Next morning I fled. I locked the house, took the ferry across to Mamoudzou with Bosco and on the jetty, on the other side, I waited for La Teigne.

Bruce

You're the only one does any talking, and you talk well, yeah, that you do, coming out with those nice clean, tidy, French words, nice white words. Well, look at you now. What good did all that do, if you ended up here?

I'm looking at you now and I hate you like I did when I was alive. I hear every word you say, even when your mouth is shut and your eyes are closed, I hear them and now I'm the one telling a story.

La Teigne told me about you, he told me he'd met a black *muzungu* but he thought you were African, a proper negro, one of them who wears shirts and pants and speaks French, not one of them dying in the gutter in Rwanda, the Congo or Somalia. He said you followed him everywhere like a dog, that you put your hand into your pocket without a second thought and you were called Mo and had a weird eye. *Weird*, that's the word he used, the dumb bastard.

I can tell you now that we made us a film, La Teigne, Rico and me. We said we were going to take you along with us, give you stuff to smoke and then kidnap you and demand cash from your African mother and father who speak French and drive to work in posh black Nissans with smoked glass windows. We were going to nab you coming out of school. *Watch out for my cousin* La Teigne said. *I don't give a shit about your cousin* I said. We were going to lock you up in the *banga* up on the hill and tie you up so tight you couldn't move. What are you worth, Moïse? So that's your real name is it, Mo-ïse, a name it hurts your mouth to say, Mo-ïse. Everyone has their price, everything on earth has a price, anything at all, just like, say, that there bench has a price, that cop just now, he has a price, and you have a price too and we told ourselves we were going to work out what your price was by watching you carefully. La Teigne was on the case, he'd learned that you lived alone with your mother, so your price went up, my dear Mo-ïse, you were your *maman*'s darling, she'd pay lots of dollars, lots of cash, money money money but . . .

You came to us, my little darlin'. You were waiting with your dog in the parking lot by the market, I don't know what you did to get a mutt as ugly as that, we'd been watching you for a good while, we're at home there, that's our turf.

We watched you all day you know. If you knew all the things you can learn about a person just quietly watching them! You were waiting in the shade, you can't handle sunlight, I guess your *maman* has shielded you all your life, with sunscreen and all that. Not for a second did you take off that fucking cap of yours with NY on it. What is NY anyway? A band? A shop? You went and walked around in the market several times. You came back with a bag and a few bananas you ate in the shade. You gave some to your stinking dog, you fed him with your fingers, for fuck's sake, that's disgusting. You drank two bottles of water, you went and had a piss at Caribou Café and got a *pain au chocolat*. You went up the hill as far as the bookshop and spent a long time looking in the window rocking your head from side to side, I don't know what you were doing. You came back to the parking lot, you waited some more and then you went and bought a roast chicken sandwich, half of which you ate and, fuck me, you gave the other half to your dog. That was when I knew what kind of a guy you were. The kind that's blind to poverty, takes holidays, has A/C in his bedroom and overflowing trash cans, the kind that's never known hunger, and doesn't know where he's from, the kind that's forgotten he's black. If you'd been within reach I'd've smashed your face in. In the afternoon you hung around some more, I thought you'd go back on the ferry but you changed your mind, you bought another *pain au chocolat*, when would you tire of filling your face? Then you went and sat down. In the afternoon the police came on the scene, a couple of them in a car together, just like two homos, they got out and as for all the kids hanging around the market and the cars, *hey presto*, they all vamoosed. But you stayed there squatting down, stroking your dog, waiting.

You're not scared of the law, of course. You're a real *muzungu*, of course you are. People were beginning to be around, the offices were closing, the market too and I gave the sign. La Teigne came down the hill, I followed him and, hey, when you saw La Teigne I thought you were going to leap into his arms or kiss him, something like that. Then I saw your eye for the first time and I wanted to kick La Teigne's ass. Why hadn't he noticed you've got one green eye! For fuck's sake! The eye of the djinn!

You see, Mo, you shouldn't believe everything you see, or that I was worth nothing. Forget all the crap you hear about what those fools in charities and NGOs and Christian rescue committees call unaccompanied minors, those people don't know a thing.

Me, I was born here. Of all the kids here I'm the only real Mahorian from Mayotte, I've got my papers. Whatever you want, I've got them all, birth certificate, identity card, even a French passport. Back home we'd say our prayers at the mosque and then went and left bottles of eau de cologne on the djinn's stone at Longoni. My father told me a woman possessed by a djinn always gives birth to weird children. Either they're very hairy, or very tall, or they've got green eyes. It's a great gift but it can be a great curse for someone who doesn't know how to use it. You see, I believe in those things, I watch the sky to check if the bats aren't flying too low, I watch the sea to see if it hasn't turned brown, I watch the color of other people's eyes, I watch to see if they have lots of hair on their arms. Those beliefs are handed down from father to son and that's how my father lives on in me, as well as my father's father and my ancestors, the original ones, the slaves. I'm not ashamed to say I'm descended from slaves. I don't spend my time moaning like you, asking myself why me, why are things like this, what have I done.

I pulled La Teigne backward and asked you *What do you want?* Your dog began to growl and I had to make an effort not to kick it in the teeth. You answered *So who are you?*

Ha, ha. You dumb bastard.

La Teigne began speaking half in French and half in Shimaore, it was all rubbish. I told La Teigne to chill. Then I answered *My name's Bruce and I'm the Don of Gaza.* You looked at me with one dark eye and one green eye and let me tell you, what's it to me now I'm dead, my heart began beating very fast. Inside my head my thoughts were spinning, going off like fireworks and I couldn't catch hold of any of them, it was all going off *wham wham wham*, your eye made me confused. My hands went up to my head, my fingers grabbed my hair and I began twisting the curls this way and that which calmed me down. I needed a smoke to collect my thoughts. It makes my mouth water just thinking about it. Need a smoke. This spliff, I could see it coming toward me in slow motion just like in the films, I'd've swallowed it whole, I love it so much, but no, easy does it, that first puff, easy does it *Sssh* when I inhale *Foooo* when I let go. Out of habit I felt in my pockets. As usual they were empty. You said *I've got money.* The ferry was coming. I heard the siren in the distance once, twice.

I've got money.

The siren sounded a third time, it woke me up and I said *We're out of here.*

Moïse

La Teigne was in front, Bosco and me in the middle, Bruce brought up the rear. I had no idea what I was doing, where I was going. I'd been waiting there all day and nobody, not one woman, not one man, not one cop had asked me what I was doing there with a dog. I was tired and lost but I knew I didn't want to go back to the house. Marie. On the ground. The smell. The rodents. The ants in the cereal. The sour milk. The noises. Bosco howling. The emptiness of the night. No.

We crossed the market square, people were coming out of everywhere and walking in all directions. There was all this noise ringing in my head, in my stomach. We branched off to the right and walked along on quite a narrow low wall that ran between the road and the mangrove swamp. The mangrove plants grew in earth or black sand, I don't know which. All along next to the low wall on the swamp side there were plastic bags, old shoes, toys, worn-out mattresses, colored electric cables. The sun was setting and, in this light, as it turned blue-gray at first, then dark gray, I was beginning to feel oppressed. I felt so vulnerable, so small, edging along in this half-light with Bosco's fluorescent yellow leash clasped in my hands. Very quickly night descended upon us like a thick blanket. The sound of engines. The explosive noise of motor-bikes. Shouts, I couldn't tell if they were friendly or threatening. Impassive faces suddenly lit up by headlights. People walking in the same direction as us or the other way, back toward Mamoudzou.

I didn't dare speak, I didn't dare look back to see if Bruce was still behind me, all I did was concentrate on where I was putting my feet. I don't know which I was more terrified of, falling over to the left under the wheels of a car or tumbling down to the right into the dirty black sandy earth of the mangrove swamp. Yet I went on because each time I felt like turning back I reminded myself of what lay in wait for me, over there, in the house on Petite-Terre.

We'd reached Kaweni, on the outskirts of Mamoudzou. Now on both sides of the road there were businesses, factories, restaurants and finally a bit of sidewalk, streetlamps. We went on without hurrying, through the noise, the dust. What was I thinking? Nothing, really. I looked around and went on walking, as if I had no choice but to keep putting one foot in front of the other, drawn forward by La Teigne, thrust on from behind by Bruce. I walked.

At a junction, Bruce suddenly crossed the road and went to talk to some homeboys sitting quietly under a streetlamp. Then he came back toward us, his face expressionless. He asked me how much I had, I replied *Fifty*. I thrust my hands into my pockets and took out two coins as well, one of two euros and the other twenty centimes. So then I said *Fifty-two euros and twenty centimes*. Bruce started laughing and the thought struck me that he really had a lot of teeth and they were very white. He held out his hand and I gave it all to him, the two coins bundled up in the notes. He crossed the road again and went up to the homeboys. Under the yellow light from the streetlamp the boys rose to their feet and in one brisk movement sucked in Bruce. I looked at La Teigne who was staring at the spot where Bruce had disappeared into the midst of the group. His arms were crossed and his face was impassive, he didn't look like he was fifteen, he looked like a man without fear. I told myself I should do the same, contract my facial muscles, fold my arms and stare at a fixed point.

I can remember those long minutes when the cars were speeding past, engines roaring. There were motorbikes coming and going and men endlessly walking along both sides of the road and beneath the streetlamp, on the far side, the home-boys stood there, looking around, motionless, showing no emotion. Bosco was pressed up against my ankles, I sensed him trembling a bit, I gently stroked his left flank and I could feel his soft skin shifting across his bones. I whispered *Bosco Bosco good dog* with the thought that these words might perhaps remind him of the house, the terrace where he liked to sleep in the shade and the long grass in the summer where he liked to play.

Suddenly the headlights of a car picked out the figure of Bruce on the far side of the road. He was holding a plastic bag in his hand. I wondered how long he'd been standing there watching me stroking Bosco, for I was convinced it was me he was watching, not La Teigne, not the passing cars, not the people still walking past, not the flashing sign for the mobile phone company that was behind us. I felt as if I'd been caught doing something wrong and I straightened up abruptly, my heart suddenly beating faster. Bosco stood up as well, growling.

We went over to him and made our way into Gaza. I don't know who it was that gave the name Gaza to the Kaweni neighborhood, I'm not sure I know where the real city of Gaza is, but I know it's not good. Even if that person had given this place a nice name, one not evocative of war and dead children, a name like Tahiti, redolent of flowers, a name like Washington, redolent of broad avenues and people in suits and ties, a name like California, redolent of sunshine and girls, would that have changed the lives and the mindset of the people living there?

That evening Gaza was all black and white. The white of the little boys' tunics on their way to prayers or coming home, the black of the gutters I was afraid of falling into, the white of the plastic pails and bottles lined up near the standpipes, the black faces and whites of eyes. I breathed in the smell of Mayotte's Gaza and I now know, without ever having travelled, that it's the smell of all the ghettos in the world. The sour urine on street corners, ancient shit in the gutters, chicken being grilled on top of old oil drums, eau de cologne and spices outside the houses, the sour sweat of men and women and musty reek of limp laundry. The constant noise that drowns out all thoughts, all memories, all dreams. The music from cars passing with open windows and, spilling out from every floor in all the buildings, the muezzin's call to prayer, a TV weather forecast, the shouts of children at play, the crying of hungry babies too famished to sleep, and I walked along in the middle of it all, holding Bosco's leash gripped in my hand as if, without it, I'd be the one to slip into a dark gutter brimming with who knows what. I followed Bruce who moved like a dancer, darting here, swerving there, then going off at a tangent. He went into a garage, there was a dirty yellow light bulb in the ceiling, half of a car on a dark floor, a smell of gasoline and metal that set my teeth on edge. In the corner a man was chewing a piece of cassava, I could hear his teeth crunch-crunching away at this hard root and from the height of my fourteen years I wanted to say to him *Cassava has to be eaten cooked, you need to boil it first*. He didn't even look up at us. We walked out again and strode down into a gully. Bruce didn't once look around to see where I was, maybe he wanted to shake me off, but I'd never been so focused and agile. My feet sank into something soft and oozing, it was the bed of the gully but it wasn't water flowing there. I glanced either side of me, there were a few lights here and there, a brazier further down and shadowy figures above the flames, but we had to keep going, we were on sloping ground, it was slippery under my sneakers and it stank, I smelled of shit, I stumbled, there was a fragment of rock like a dagger going into my knee but, like the others, I kept my mouth shut and went on climbing. The noise had faded, the smells of the ghetto subsided, when I held out my hand I could touch leaves, branches, my heart was pounding in my chest. I was afraid but at the same time I was excited.

Bosco was running at my side, his yellow leash glowed in the darkness, and I was climbing up toward Gaza's sky, without knowing who or what awaited me.

We ended up in front of a *banga* and Bruce opened the door and went in. Suddenly everything had become very calm, Bruce and La Teigne sat down on mattresses on the ground. Rico, another guy, came in and settled down as well. There was a light bulb in the ceiling and an electric cable dangled, forming a U in the air and disappearing into the darkness. My jeans were torn, there was blood and mud on them, my sneakers were black with filth. We drank Oasis, tropical flavor, straight from the bottle. I asked for water for Bosco and the boys stared at me as if they hadn't understood what I'd just said. Then Bruce nudged La Teigne with his elbow and he got up and disappeared into the hut's other room. He came back with a Coke bottle filled with water and half a coconut shell. I held the coconut shell in front of Bosco's nose for him to drink and the three boys watched me, openmouthed, as if fascinated. Bruce asked *Does he bite, your dog?* I replied *No, not at all, he's very friendly.* Then Bruce laughed the way he had earlier and said *Hey, that's a pity!* La Teigne started laughing as well, emitting a metallic sound from his mouth and I asked myself how it was that I'd never heard this before, but I think La Teigne had never laughed before and when Bruce stopped laughing he fell quiet at once. We divided up two baguettes and a tin of tuna between us. I gave half of my portion to Bosco. Bruce asked me *Do you share everything with your dog?* I replied *Yes of course, he has to eat,* and this time Bruce didn't laugh, he just looked at me nodding his head and repeating my words *He has to eat, he has to eat.*

After that they put on some American rap with lots of words like *nigga fuck ghetto.* Bruce liked these words a lot. I thought for a moment about the *mgodro* music my friend Moussa liked listening to, but that memory seemed to come from another era. While the music played Bruce emptied three cigarettes onto a sheet of paper. The tobacco formed a neat mound like a miniature hill. Then he took a little package out of the plastic bag and undid it with great care. Inside it there were three pills. He put them beside the mound. He took out another package, a larger one that he undid very carefully. This contained some grass. I remember Bruce's nimble fingers and how they moved very gracefully from one heap to another. He crushed the pills with the handle of a machete, then he drew the blade across the powder several times with regular movements to make the powder lie evenly. He scattered tobacco, grass and powder from the white pills onto some cigarette papers. He did it like a chef, a pinch of this a pinch of that. La Teigne was on his feet, jumping up and down on the spot and from time to time Bruce gave him a look and he calmed down for a moment. He rolled several spliffs and handed me one, saying *This is Papa Bruce's good spice* and when I thanked him he inclined his head in an exaggerated bow and said *No, thanks to you Mo.* La Teigne and Rico repeated *Thanks to you Mo.*

First off I watched them smoking, then I lit my spliff, I remember Bosco going *eee-eee-eee* and maybe my dog was trying to tell me something, but I put the spliff to my lips and inhaled. After that I toppled over, head first, into another world.

I'm lying there and Marie's looking down at me, she's saying *Wake up Moïse, you're going to be late for school.*

I'm lying there and I can hear Bosco scratching at the door. I say to Marie, *He's hungry,* but Marie isn't there it's Bruce who's there, saying to me *Oh yes he has to eat.* Then he starts laughing.

Now I'm on my feet and chanting words I don't understand. *Nigga nigga nigga nananana fuck fuck fuck nananana.* La Teigne is on the ground, laughing his metallic laughter and I go up to him and say, *nigga nigga nigga.* He's still laughing. I kick him in the ribs. He laughs more than ever.

I piss outside, I shit outside and a woman walks by. It's not Marie, it's someone I don't know. The sun fills the sky and it's so hot I strip off my clothes. The woman starts yelling.

I'm still smoking and drinking Oasis that has a funny taste. I'm drinking from Bosco's half coconut shell, but Bosco's not there, I call him but my dog doesn't appear, he must be sulking. That's what Marie used to say when he didn't want to show himself, *Bosco's sulking.* All at once I hear my own voice, is it me, is it someone else, is it a memory? *Mam! Mam!* And I want to get out of the *banga* but I can't, there are no doors, no windows.

I'm on my feet and I'm reciting. "When I was still very young we lived in the country. Our house was no more than a small leasehold farm, standing isolated in an expanse of fields. There we spent a peaceful existence. My parents had living

64

with them my father's great-aunt, Aunt Martine." Bruce starts laughing and I chant *Aunt Martine fuck Aunt Martine Aunt Martine iz a nigga,* and I rap just like I was the greatest rapper of all time. Mo Tupac Mo Jay Z Mo Dr. Dre. And Bruce is laughing so much that he cries. And I, Moïse, I'm fourteen years old, I'm smoking, I'm drinking, I'm rapping and dancing with my pals, I have no past, no future, I'm happy.

Bruce

I wish you'd shut up, just shut the fuck up, I know your mouth's closed but I can still hear you loud and clear and the whole tale you're telling is coming straight at me like that bullet in the woods when you shot me. I wonder where my body is now, is it still up there? You left me there the way you left your mother lying rotting, your mother being devoured by rats as big as cats and her body swollen like a balloon and the stink, do you remember the stink, you who talk about Gaza the way all whiteys talk about Gaza, you talk about shit you talk about garbage you talk about poverty like all those journalists who come to our turf the way they go to the pictures, then afterwards they write big words like *the biggest shantytown on Mayotte* or like *a garbage dump open to the skies*. You do the same. You talk and think just like that.

You should've known how it was before, that gully filled with shit you're talking about. A tall, green forest's what it was, a forest my father my mother my brothers and I visited every week. I don't have words like you Mo, I don't have big phrases in my head but I often think about those years. I'm eight-nine-ten, I live in my father's house on the slopes of Mamoudzou. I'm never hungry, I go to the French school every day and in the evening I go to the madrasa. At the French school I learn *Je suis tu es il/elle/on est nous sommes vous êtes ils/elles sont* and the teachers are elegant white women and they say you're French *Allons enfants de la patrie* and they don't use a stick to hit you with when you do something wrong no they stroke your head and say you little devil. At the madrasa we dress in white and we recite the Quran and if you make a mistake *thwack* you get hit by a branch from a mango tree but it's not too bad that's how life is and they say to us you're Muslims and that's how I live, I'm Mahorian, I'm French, I'm a Muslim what do I know about it I never go hungry. I'm the only one of my father's children to go to school because I'm the youngest and my father has asked the djinn on the hill to watch over me. I go and play with my friends. I go and eat at my friends' houses, I climb the coconut palms and the mango trees, I never go hungry, I bathe in the gully and my mother and my aunts washing their laundry there tell me to bathe higher up but I like the smell of soap and the water turning white so I bathe and my skin itches and peels from the bars of soap bought at Sodifram but I never go hungry.

It's Friday and I'm on the lookout behind the door for my father. I'm wearing my fine tunic embroidered with threads of gold and I'm waiting for my father who arrives in his fine Friday tunic as well and we're going to see the djinn. We walk down the gully, we cross over the clear water that goes *slap slap slap* against the rocks that are still white from soap and my father says *Hoist up your tunic* and I hoist up my tunic and we climb up as far as the orchard and my father says *Hush*

67

and I walk softly and I'm proud to be with him, there's nothing here apart from fruit trees and lianas and trees so vast that they make me a little afraid. My father takes a small pot of honey and an egg out of his bag and puts them down beside a tall tree. *It's for the Wanaisas* he says *Do you know who they are?* I answer him with what I've learned at the Koranic school. *The Wanaisas are little hairy men with their feet pointing the other way each with a missing left arm who protect the forest and the riverbeds.* My father looks at me and smiles. He shows me trees, he tells me never to pick those fruits after nightfall and, *There,* he points again, and as he raises his arm like that to point to the tops of the trees his tunic falls back so his fine wristwatch can be seen *There, that tree must never be cut down, even if it's diseased it must be left to die here and it will turn into dust and the Wanaisas will use the dust and another tree, even finer, will take its place.*

We walk slowly and I like watching the water gushing down between the two flights of stone steps. These steps are so old that they were already there when my father was a child. My father won't allow me to dive in here but all my friends go there. I watch them, they say to me, *Come on in scaredy-cat* but I never go there, I've given my word, Mo, I watch them climbing up the steps and leaping into the pool shouting and laughing but I never go in. Beyond the steps there are more trees and further on a big green pool. Then my father brings out the bottle of eau de cologne, some milk and cakes. The water's as green as your frigging eye that's brought me bad luck and my father prays and kneels on the ground his tunic gets dirty and I know my mother will wash it the next day, going *ttt* with pursed lips but my father doesn't care. Every Friday my father and me go to see the djinn and my father asks him to watch over me, he prays for me to go far for me to cross the seas for me to wear a suit and tie for me to speak good French and write good French for me one day to work in an office, he says all that my poor father. My father warns me *This djinn is watching you, this djinn has its eye on you and the evil that you do to it, it will do to you in return and the good that you do to it, it will do to you in return* and when I was little I used to keep looking over my shoulder but I didn't jump into the pool with my friends because the djinn was watching every one of my actions.

I'm eight-nine-ten and my name is Ismaël Saïd. I like listening to the bats in the trees and I picture myself flying like them, hanging upside down and seeing another world, maybe that's stupid but that's how my thoughts are. One day in a group arranged by the *muzungus* that was called "The Children of Mayotte" they showed us the film *Batman* and that's the moment when I realize that I'm Bruce Wayne, I feel him within myself, I copy his voice, I copy his anger and I want to paint everything black and have a cape and all that crap.

I'm eight-nine-ten and I don't go hungry, but I don't have enough exercise books and I don't understand everything *J'ai tu as il/elle/a nous avons vous avez ils/elles ont* I don't understand proper nouns and the nouns that are not proper and I get tired in class because it's so hot in the room in my father's house where we sleep that I can never get to sleep and I don't have enough time and I'm not clever enough so say the teachers who are elegant and white and the headmaster says the same thing to my father who's silent from shame. That day he's wearing his dark cotton trousers and his shirt with blue stripes and he hasn't put his embroidered *kofia* on his head to go to see the French people and my father thinks he's having a meeting about my transfer to secondary school, and before even getting there he's full of pride but the headmaster says *No this school doesn't suit him he finds it hard he's not happy here, he wouldn't be happy at secondary school* and the headmaster gives him the name of a special school for children with serious learning difficulties. I'll never forget that *with serious learning difficulties* and he says *Ismaël will do better there* and my father turns to me and in his eyes something is broken. I begin shouting, I'd like to leap onto the desk and grab the headmaster by the throat but he stands up and says *You can see for yourself, Monsieur, secondary school wouldn't suit him.*

I'm eight-nine-ten and I refuse to go to this school for the disabled. I weep I yell my father beats me my mother beats me but I refuse to be with people who drool and spend the whole day drawing and every afternoon I go to wait for the headmaster because I want to talk to him to make him change his mind but when I see him I want to thump him I want to thump his family and one day I throw a stone that hits him in the back then another and a third and after that I lose track.

I'm ten-eleven and I steal one euro from my big sister's purse. My father ties me to a chair and every member of the family comes and slaps me once or twice. My father says that if I start again he'll tie me up in the village square. That no longer affects me, I'm not a little boy anymore I'm no longer Ismaël Saïd my name is Bruce now, I jump into the pool, I run around all day, I sleep under the veranda decks of strange houses and I go hungry. Someone, I don't know who, gives me a cigarette and a Coke, then a cigarette and a beer. I steal fruits and sell them to illegal immigrants who set up stalls by the roadside and sell them on. I go hungry, my mother feeds me in secret but in my father's house I'm always in a rage, it's as if an evil djinn enters me as soon as I cross the threshold and I strike out, I yell.

I'm ten-eleven and the corrugated iron huts are starting to appear one after another. Illegal immigrants coming and building them where it shouldn't happen, where the Wanaisas live, they dig holes, they make fires, they lay down pipes to collect water from the pools and they shit everywhere and the pool dries up and nobody jumps in there anymore because there's no water left and no one washes their laundry anymore and the water smells of shit and piss and gasoline. The forest's dying and in its place there are tinsmiths covering the earth with iron and fire.

I steal here and there, I win a couple of times in the *mourengué* fights, I become strong, I become dangerous, I want to hit anything that moves. I'm twelve-thirteen my prick itches and I want a woman but for a woman you need euros and one day I steal my father's watch and I go see the *sousou* girls at the Cavani crossroads and I fuck for the first time in the mangrove swamp. When I go home, my father's waiting for me at the bottom of the village but I'm a man now, I've fucked and my name is Bruce and I'm not afraid and I dance around him the way I do in the *mourengué* fights and he looks at me with that same broken look and it's all over.

I'm fourteen-fifteen I'm on the streets and all day I hang around, I drink, I smoke. When I haven't got enough money for the *sousous* I go with the other homeboys to steal goats and fuck them, it's not the same but it calms you down. At night I stalk and rob and make decent people like my father jump he's left his house and now lives up north and I know how and who to rob and I know who sells what, I know who buys, I barricade the streets when I want to and I've only to say the word and it's war. When there are elections you've seen how they eat out of my hand, you've seen how they seek me out, where's Bruce, what does Bruce think, what's Bruce doing. The king of Gaza, that's me.

I wonder where they're going to bury me and what name they're going to give me. I wonder if they're going to notify my father by telling him *Your son Ismaël Saïd is dead* or if they'll tell him *Bruce is dead* he won't understand a thing and all this fuckries is because of you.

Moïse

There was nothing left to smoke, nothing left to drink, nothing left to eat. I was on the ground, it felt like my mouth was full of earth. There was nobody around in the *banga*. I crawled over to the door and outside the sunlight transfixed my eyes, the yellow light bored into my head with the noise of a power drill. Somehow or other I found a barrel filled with water, I plunged my head into it again and again. I drank more and more from the water I'd just plunged my head into with my filthy face. I was barefoot. Maybe if I'd stayed a little longer, alone on that dry, red hillside, outside that corrugated iron *banga*, maybe if I'd looked around me and seen that Gaza was no more than a collection of huts stained red with dust, tangled electric cables, and corrugated iron roofs held in place by big rocks, if I'd seen that there would never be any way out for me, if I'd understood that these footpaths and alleyways held no good for me, then maybe I'd have run back to Mamoudzou as fast as I could, back to the ferry, back to the house, back to Marie's lifeless body. But while I was washing myself Bruce appeared and behind him were La Teigne, Rico, and a couple of other homeboys I didn't know. These two looked like they were barely ten years old. Bruce said *We're out of here.* I said *Where are we going?* My voice was hoarse, the words stuck in my throat. Bruce didn't reply.

We walked down the hill single file. We were walking toward Mamoudzou, I looked at the clock in front of the landing stage, it showed twenty past one but I didn't know what day it was and I still don't know how much time I'd spent up there. Bruce bought tickets for the six of us and it was only at that moment that I thought about Bosco. I asked La Teigne *Where's my dog?* He shrugged. When we got on the ferry I went up to Bruce and asked him the same question and he answered *You take care of the money and you'll see your dog later.* I began to be scared and I asked *What money?* Bruce came up to me, he was wearing clean clothes, his breath was fresh. La Teigne, Rico, and the two kids were the same, as if freshly washed. I was the only one who was dirty and stinking. Bruce put a hand on my leg. *You said your mother had some cash at her house and you knew her* carte bleue *pin number and you said we should go to your house, didn't you, don't you remember, you said that only this morning so we've washed and got ourselves spruced up to go and call on your* maman, *haven't you noticed?* While he was talking he was squeezing my thigh harder and harder. The people around us noticed nothing, they were chatting, laughing, drowsing, or looking at the sea. How was it that no one noticed I was scared? Scared of Bruce, scared of going back to the house, scared of everything, it was a feeling that overwhelmed me, kept me from thinking, from running away, from doing anything other than stay there sitting on that wooden bench, staring at the sea without seeing it, watching

Petite-Terre draw closer, recognizing the corrugated iron shelter on the landing stage where I'd waited for Marie so many times, still feeling so totally terrified that I ended up feeling that fear is all I am, all I have, feeling that fear is my very name.

We took a taxi, just as if we were boys from school, and in the cab Bruce joked with the others in Shimaore and the driver joined in their laughter.

Bruce stationed one kid at the corner of the road that led to my house and another one fifty yards lower down. I'd found the bunch of keys in my pocket. It had stayed there since the day I ran away from the house with Bosco. How was that possible? I was shaking as I opened the padlock to the little iron gate that led to the garden. Bruce ordered Rico to wait beside the gate. We walked along the right-hand side of the house. I was shaking without being able to stop myself and it took me several attempts to open the padlock on the big gate to the terrace. La Teigne sniffed noisily and Bruce said *It stinks here.* My teeth were chattering as the chain fell at my feet with a big crash. Everything swam before my eyes and Bruce said *Fuck me, what's that smell?*

The buzzing of the flies. Bruce giving me a kick in my back and talking in Shimaore, I'm on the ground, I'm afraid, I cling to his ankles, I don't know why, the smell's unbearable and he yells *Where's the cash, where's the cash?* as he's struggling to break free. I crawl up to Marie's bedroom where everything's as perfect and white as before, but the smell of death lurks there too, I catch sight of her dark brown rucksack and check that her wallet is inside it, I go into my room, I pick up my book and want to stay there. I'll shut myself in here in this white perfection and in the end the smell will go away. One of the kids outside gives a yell and Bruce bursts in on me, tries to snatch the bag from my grasp but I resist and then he grips me by the throat and I'm outside.

I hear a car pulling up on the gravel outside the house, I hear a shout *The police!* and we're running, climbing over metal fences, leaping into other gardens, and we're running and running, grass asphalt mud earth stones cement beneath my feet barking shouting car horns squealing brakes the muezzin my own panting in my ears, I'm scratched hit punch drunk beaten pushed thrust aside but I'm running and I'm putting a distance between myself and the house and I know I'll never go back there.

When we came to a halt it was in the woods on Moya Hill. Beyond its farthest slope lay Moya Beach and the memory of Sunday afternoons with Marie, but that was when I was a child, when I thought I was white, when I thought she'd be staying with me all my life. I gave all the money to Bruce, I promised him next day I'd go and get more notes from the cash machine. I emptied the rucksack in front of him, he divided up all the stuff and took what he wanted: what was left was Marie's identity card, her silk scarf, and the book, *The Boy and the River*. I thrust them into the bag.

Night was beginning to fall. I was scared but I stuck close to Bruce.

Bruce

I guess you think it's easy to be the Don of Gaza.

You don't get to be king just like that, it's a jungle out here, you need to be a lion, a wolf, you need to sniff the air, track down your prey and show your claws. I showed mine at the time of the big strikes. Who lit the first bonfire at the Kaweni crossroads? Me. Who decided to put up barricades? Me. Who threw the first stone at the firemen? Me. Ha, ha. Everyone took my lead, adults, civil servants, street vendors, the unions, they all shouted *No to high prices!* but I couldn't give a shit what they were shouting, the one who'd lit the fire was me and that's what makes a warlord, he leads the pack, he lights the fire and, when he decides, he puts out the fire himself. And everyone knew that. I heard the wind speaking to me with the voices of people everywhere. *It was Bruce who barricaded the Kaweni road, it was Bruce who decided, it was Bruce who said the word, you need to ask Bruce, where's Bruce?* Even the wind spoke my name and it was like Gotham summoning up Batman.

You need to know Gaza like it was your wife. You know where she's wrinkled, where she's curvaceous, you know when she's crying out and when she's in pain, you know what she likes and what she doesn't like, you know what music she likes, you know how to please her and how to make her grovel, you know where she's dry and where she's dripping wet. You know her head from her pussy, and her hands from her feet. No one knows Gaza like me.

You need to be strong, you mustn't be scared to fight. In Gaza they know Bruce is like Batman, he dominates everyone. He doesn't grovel either to the law or to politicians. He can turn anything into a weapon, a stone, a stick, a sheet of corrugated iron, the lid of a cooking pot. You need to know how to strike and you need everyone to see you win.

What you did to me yesterday I'll never forgive and neither will my wolves.

You need to have an army. Youths to keep watch on all sides, and you send them to beg from the *muzungus*. You set up competitions between them, you send some to Caribou Café, some to the exit from the ferry and some to Banana Café, then you wait. They come back to Gaza smiling as if you'd invented the most wonderful game for them. Do you think you could have thought up that game, fool? Youths are useful too for climbing all over the place, into trees for fruit, onto roofs when you want to pinch a TV cable, that kind of thing.

You need your homies your age to help and protect you. The hardest part is choosing them. They need to be strong, but not as strong as you, brave but not as brave as you, they need to respect you enough to follow you and even die for you, you must know their secrets, their vices, their little weaknesses. I'd seen your secret and your weakness. You left your mother to snuff it on the kitchen floor and you're a scaredy-cat. You put us in danger that day, didn't you, Monsieur Mo-ïse who said he had money at his house but didn't tell anyone there was a body quietly rotting on the kitchen floor and for that you had to pay, that's how it is if you want to be in Bruce's gang, you've got to prove yourself, you've got to give blood. If you didn't want that you shouldn't have stayed all night at my place and followed me like a dog. You shouldn't have begged me not to leave you there at Moya, you little homo.

To be king you need to have people on your side, ones you'll give a cigarette to, a spliff, a piece of advice, protection, and who, in return, tell you things. Tell you who's leaving Gaza, who's coming back to Gaza, who's saying things about you, what they're saying about you. Tell you what houses are empty for the holidays, what warehouses have had fresh deliveries. What you do is you listen, you listen carefully, you listen to everyone, even to the ones who tell you nothing but bullshit because you never know and then you use your head.

Most of all you need to have the dough, cash, moolah, money money money, you need it coming in and going out, you need it to get drunk and to get high, stuff needs to be sold on. You need to be the one who has the best spliff and the one who shares it with the others. You need to be the one who has the best sound and when Saturday night comes around people need to hear *boom boom* from your system, and they need to know it's coming from your place.

For you to stay on top, hang on in there, the rules need to keep changing. No one should get used to Gaza and stop being scared. Even if there was money at your place, even if the *carte bleue* worked for a couple of days and I was able to get a decent stash of cash, you put us in danger and the law got on our tail. To stay Don you have to punish, and I punished. I'm not like you, I don't open my mouth to say nice things, to say *I'm sorry I'm very sorry*. No, I speak the truth. Three days after that trip to your place you felt like you were my brother, didn't you? You started talking as if you knew better than everyone else, you said you didn't like stealing, you didn't want to smoke or drink anymore and for a couple of days I let you carry on. You even started talking to me the way the guys from the NGOs talk to me. *Why do you do it Bruce? Why don't you want to change your way of life? Why do you live a life of violence?* You told me the story of your life and, for fuck's sake, I don't know how I stopped myself from smashing in your face that day. You told me how your mother, your real mother, that whore, gave you to the *muzungu* woman and how that one got a certificate of paternity for you. You told me how happy you were with her, you used that word *happy*, like the whites, like in schoolbooks, like those elegant white teachers and the headmaster who told my father *He's not happy here, he wouldn't be happy at secondary school* and I thought it was the djinn who'd sent you with your eye as green as the trees they live in and that I needed to do something to stop you talking like that about school and your picnics by Lake Dziani *Your favorite place in the world* but what fucking world are you living in? This is Mayotte here and you say it's France. Fuck off! Is France like this? In France do you see

children hanging around the streets from dawn to d
you? In France are there scores of *kwassa-kwassas* an
with people landing on beaches, some of them already half
dead? In France are there people who live all their lives in
the woods? In France do people cover their windows with
iron grilles like here? In France do people shit and sling their
trash into gullies like they do here?

I'm the king and I needed to punish you, Mo. I needed
to change the rules, I needed to show that when it comes to
people like you, with skins as black as mine but whose words
are white and insipid like those of the *muzungus*, I needed to
show I knew how to settle the score with people like that.

I put out the word in Gaza. On Saturday night there's going
to be *mourengué* fighting on the hill. On Saturday it's punish-
ment time. I've seen my father doing *mourengué* fighting, I've
seen my uncles, my cousins, and, in my dreams, I see my ancestors battling and dancing in the ring formed by the crowd.
Saturday came. The drums were set up. There were drinks and
cigarettes. There was dancing, there was bare-handed fighting
the way we Mahorians know how to do it. When I came into
the ring the drumming grew faster and I was stripped to the
waist while you still had your old T-shirt on and you were
already stoned out of your mind, you'd been smoking too
much and you were laughing and all at once I jumped on you,
I can't say you didn't defend yourself it was simply amazing,
you amazed me, Mo, you kicked out, you flung your hands
about but you didn't know how to fight while dancing around,
you didn't know how to be both strong and light, you didn't

81

know how to call the ancestors to help you, and didn't know how to follow the rhythm of the drums. You didn't know how to imitate Muhammad Ali when he leaps into the ring and he's so light on his feet that you think he's going to kiss you but *bang bang* that's how I jumped on you and when you began yelling, your green eye opened wide like never before and in it I saw my father, I saw the djinns, I saw this hill before Gaza existed, I saw my childhood and the green of the trees and the fruits that mustn't be picked at nightfall and the leaves that mustn't be touched and I made a sign and my machete appeared in my hand and I drew it across your face from above the eyebrow down to the jaw like that, the way you draw a pencil across paper, gently but firmly the elegant white teachers used to say, without pressing, without hesitating, a fine, firm line and the blood pissed out the crowd yelled, and I felt the weight of the king of Gaza's golden crown on my head I'm not lying. I don't open my mouth to tell lies, but you didn't cry out you didn't move maybe you didn't feel anything, after all you're the child of the djinn and my father had told me to beware of the djinn.

What's the time? At this hour of the day I'm often in my *banga* or underneath the breadfruit tree behind the tinsmith's workshop. I like people to come to me if they need to but I shouldn't be seen too much. I listen to music, smoke a little but not too much, I collect the money from the youths, I figure out our weekend plan of action. It's in the evening that I go down to the entrance to Gaza. Ah, Mo, it gives me a hard-on sometimes, to know they're all afraid of me, to see them all

salivating over the notes in my pocket and the words com
out of my mouth and they all want to talk to me, to ask me
what I think, and want to get close to me because I'm Bruce,
king of Gaza. That's not all I wanted, I'm only seventeen for
fuck's sake, I wanted to become king of Mayotte, king of the
Comoros, I wanted my name to be on the prefect's lips, on
everyone's lips, all the *muzungus*, the sailors, the firefighters,
the bureaucrats, the law.

What's the time? It's not real life here, is it? Hey, Mo,
answer. I'll wake up and feel something again, won't I, this
wall I see myself touching, yet I can't touch it for real, it'll stop
soon, this business, Mo, tell me, I'm still king of Gaza, aren't
I? I'm telling you, I miss my hill and all my homies, I miss the
late-morning sun and the smell of the gully, I miss the metallic
smoke from the tinsmith's workshop and the *clang clang*
sounds beneath the sun and the noise of their saws and the
clatter of their hammers. I shouldn't be here, I've got to get
out of here, get back to Gaza. Back there's where I belong.

Moïse

It was an old white man called Dédé who stitched me up. He wears a loincloth and a sleeveless T-shirt and has the TV on night and day. There's a photo of him in military uniform in his living room.

I stayed at his house for several weeks. Time had ceased to matter. I'd wound up in a secret place, a dark night without end from which it would be impossible for me to escape.

Even though, according to Dédé, the cut was not deep, the scar remained pale and long, my right eyelid had collapsed so that all the time it feels as if my eye's misted over but it's simply the effect of my eyelashes. On occasion in the evening, when I was feeling bad and all that had happened to me was prowling around me like a predator ready to pounce once more, I imagined that this haziness was a supernatural and benevolent presence bringing me word from Marie and Bosco, giving me news of everything and nothing. From time to time Bruce would come and see me at nightfall. He'd stand beside the bed saying nothing and studying me. I don't know what he was looking at, maybe he was checking that I was still scared of him? The old white man changed my dressing regularly, checked the stitches, took my temperature. I had fresh clothes, new shoes, my brown rucksack was at the foot of the bed. I was allowed to move freely inside the house but I didn't have the right to leave. Dédé spoke little and when he wasn't looking after me he watched TV and drank. His daily consumption of alcohol was incredible yet he was never drunk. Sometimes when I refused to eat, he would feed me with a spoon, saying *Come on, kid, just one more* and maybe I cried a little, then, I don't know.

When Bruce came to get me, Dédé said I should come back to see him once a month. Bruce handed him a bag filled with bottles of booze, the old man closed the door without giving me another glance. I heard the sound of the TV. I'm guessing that, as with all of us, Bruce knew Dédé's dark secrets and weaknesses. I never saw him again.

When my scar irritated me, I went into the woods in search of aloe vera leaves and spread their glutinous sap over my face. I'd seen Marie doing that long ago with a scar on her leg that sometimes irritated her on humid days.

For a long time after that I didn't speak. I held everything in and my whole body became an enclosed space where I stored up words and thoughts and sometimes there was a bubbling in my stomach *pop pop pop* like rice cooking. They all said that after the *mourengué* I'd lost my mind and I let it be said, I let them talk. And maybe they were right because sometimes, very early in the morning when I was climbing right to the top of the hill of Mamoudzou, I'd utter a cry and even though I knew this cry arose from my own gut, it was so deep, dense and dark that I didn't recognize it.

For a long while after that I was a trusty soldier in Bruce's army. I kept watch when I was told to keep watch, I counted the numbers of unfamiliar cars coming into Gaza, I went out and tore up cassava roots and boiled them up, I pinched shoes and slippers from the mosque, I went and picked fruit, and stole clothes hanging out to dry on walls, I guarded Bruce's *banga* when he was away, when he was fucking, occasionally I cleaned it as well. In the daytime I kept thoughts, memories, and questions at bay. At night I would try to find a place to get a few hours' sleep but sometimes all I did was walk the streets, walking in my sleep.

One day, as I was going in search of bananas in the little plantation located above the two flights of stone steps, I came upon Bosco. For the previous two days it had been raining and Gaza seemed to be trying to cave in on itself. Whole masses of earth were coming adrift from the hillside. The tinsmith's workshop had subsided, a torrent of mud flowed through the gully. I had no idea where Bruce had gone and I was left there watching the rain, the mud and things that were slowly disintegrating and sliding down toward the sea. In my head I was praying for a void to open up where the gully was and engulf the whole of Gaza.

But the rain stopped, the sun came beating down once again and Bruce returned with his homeboys. He'd caught sight of me under the deck of the veranda of a house where the shutters and door were always closed, he called me over and said *Mo, go get some food, you'll have to manage on your own.* Since the day I'd returned to Gaza he always addressed me in firm but never aggressive tones. He simply gave me orders and I was a good dog, go, fetch, sit, on guard. I never looked him in the eye now. I kept my cap on night and day and my brown rucksack on my back.

So I'd gone up toward the top of the gully hoping to find an untouched bunch of bananas, I scrambled up as best I could, finding hand holds here and there, orientating myself from the two great black stone staircases built against the side of the hill. If those stones could speak what tales would they tell about life here before Gaza? Maybe it had been a paradise, and children came out to run and play here without fear and then went home and ate as much as they wanted and slept in clean sheets?

The path that ran along beside the banana plantation had disappeared, there was a mass of earth, scraps of metal, corrugated iron, various bits of detritus. Just as I was wondering what I should do to get to the other side I saw something yellow protruding from the ground and my heart missed a beat. It was a particular yellow that glowed in the darkness, fluorescent yellow, Marie had told me, when she bought that leash for Bosco. I thought that Bosco, whom I'd not seen again since that first evening must have been buried in a mudslide and I began tugging at it. It wouldn't come, so I dug, I scraped away with my hands, I got the leash free, saying over and over *Bosco Bosco good dog* and suddenly something emerged that was dessicated yet dripping wet, its skin cracked and torn, half skeleton, half monster, its jaws agape with the leash still attached to what was left of its neck. I didn't cry out, I didn't back away, I simply collapsed and wept there in front of Bosco who'd died a long time ago, I don't know how, but it must have been while I was smoking that first spice spliff and imitating American rappers and dancing and drinking from his coconut shell.

I'm fourteen or maybe fifteen already, I no longer know. What difference does it make after all, since every day is the same as the last. Fear, hunger, walking, sleep, hunger, fear, walking, sleep. I ate what I came across, washed when I could, slept under the decks of verandas with one eye open. I often had to keep watch at the entrance to Gaza and I collected the takings from the youths to hand on to one of Bruce's homies. On some evenings I'd see the poisonous quartet coming down the hill, Bruce surrounded by Rico, La Teigne, and Nasse. They were off on the prowl, to break into houses. I wasn't with them because, as far as they were concerned, not only was I out of my mind, but I also brought bad luck. For a long time I never went outside Gaza. For a long time I must have been dead, for I guess this is the emptiness you have in your belly and in your heart when you're dead.

One day just like the others, the same sun, the same harsh sky, the same red dust, the same *clang clang* from the workshop, the same stink of metal and shit, there was an election campaign. A youth came to fetch me. Bruce was waiting for me at his place, he was very smartly turned out, Bermuda shorts with pockets on both sides, a Lacoste polo shirt, a consular corps shoulder bag, a gold chain. He gave me fresh clothes to wear, not exactly like his own, but clean, new stuff that his soldiers steal from the illegal market that's set up every day on the edge of the mangrove swamp. There are black market street traders and black market thieves. Bruce gave me new flip-flops as well and said *You're coming with us.*

At the entrance to Gaza we mingled with the others turned out like me, smelling of deodorant and talcum powder. Bruce was in the middle, neither wholly visible nor wholly invisible. He'd only need to take one step to appear and another to disappear. A vast new car drove up with the sunlight glinting on the gray hood. Two men got out, happy and smiling. They shook hands with everyone. The taller of them went back into the vehicle and the other one, a little man with a round, friendly face, began speaking, "Young people of Kaweni, I know you are hurt by what they say about you, I know you don't like having a bad reputation. I know life's hard for you because there's no infrastructure here. There's nothing for you here, you young people, who are the future of Mayotte. If you vote for me, if you get people to vote for me, I promise they will no longer call this place Gaza but Paris! If you vote for me, if you get people to vote for me, there'll be jobs for everyone!"

We want internet! "Yes, you shall have the internet. Just look across from Ga . . . from Kaweni, just look at all those businesses, all those factories, all those supermarkets. We'll go to them, door-to-door, we'll tell them we need jobs for all our young people!"

We want identity papers! "All children born on French soil are French. All those who can prove that they have a Mahorian father with a French identity card are French. All those who don't have papers will be given residence permits because young people are our top priority!"

And so it went on. The young crowd could shout out anything at all, at one point the demand was *We want security* and the man replied, *Yes, you shall have security!* He was sweating but smiling all the time. After that he opened the trunk of his car and took out bags filled with provisions. Bruce appeared. The man looked at him, smiling, and said *Ah, there you are!* They spent a long time greeting one another. Then the man got back into his car and drove off slowly, the sunlight beaming down on the dull dust and in Bruce's hand there were banknotes. I helped to carry all the bags over to the breadfruit tree and Bruce distributed them. There was bread, sugar, flour, pasta, Coke, cookies, canned vegetables, potties for babies, diapers. Slowly, the whole of Gaza, men, women, children, babies, lined up on the two slopes of the gully and Bruce conducted the distribution smiling, in silence.

These handouts took place two or three times a week, sometimes more often, as the first round of the election drew near. Other people came, in other fine cars and some of them spoke in French, others held forth in Shimaore but they all handed out bags of provisions and money to Bruce. There was food and drink, there was money for grass, spice, cigarettes. Bruce had given orders to the youths to stay at home. Begging in Mamoudzou or down the shopping mall was now banned. As was snatching bags at the traffic lights, or stealing mobile phones at the Mamoudzou market. House break-ins had stopped, only petty thefts at the illegal market beside the mangrove swamp were tolerated. Sometimes it seemed as if even though bellies were full, even though supplies of grass made their heads sleepy, some people couldn't resist the urge to go down to the mangrove swamp and steal a T-shirt, a pair of shorts, some slippers.

After the elections the cars reverted to speeding past without stopping. The noise and fury of Gaza was roused once more. Nasse was arrested and sent back to Anjouan, La Teigne disappeared for two days and reappeared missing two fingers, the youths went back to begging, stealing and extortion, break-ins started up again, and everywhere around Kaweni metal workshops sprang up and they were all making the same things: wire mesh for windows and doors, iron bars to go inside windows and doors, sharp spikes to go on the tops of walls surrounding houses. The business of security.

It was around about this time that the smiling winner of the election set up the "Young People Forward" club in a building at the top of the hill.

Stéphane

I'm wandering around in the clubhouse, I haven't gone home, I'm looking for something, I don't know what, I'm looking for a firm hand to grasp, I'm looking for a remnant of myself to cling on to, surely there must still be a trace of the man I once was, somewhere, the one given to uttering ringing phrases like *There are no problems, only solutions* or *Where there's a will there's a way* or even *Mens sana in corpore sano?* I squeeze my body into a corner, I bang my head against the wall once, twice, I weep. I'm thinking about Moïse. Where is he right now?

Since last night when Moïse defeated Bruce in the *mourengué*, Gaza has been devouring itself from the inside. All the houses are closed up, there's not a single adult out and about, just youngsters, their eyes on fire, hands outspread, mouths open, heads cleaned out by the smoke from their spice joints. Moïse didn't just defeat Bruce, he crushed him. When he hollered his animalistic rage, expressing all of his broken life, the drums fell silent and his cry transfixed the crowd.

Where is he now? How did he manage to disappear like that, in the face of that crowd stunned at seeing their king down on the ground? There he stood, with his foot on Bruce's throat, mouth open emitting his animal cry, fist raised. Then he vanished and Bruce was still down on the ground.

I looked for him briefly but there was such tension in the air, the drummers had vanished, the crowd was hurriedly breaking up, even the little kids were following their *mamans* without a backward glance and I saw Bruce picking himself up, staggering. I couldn't see his face because he kept his head down, his hands plunged in his hair. Then I went up to the clubhouse as fast as possible. When I got there I looked to see if Moïse's brown rucksack was still buried in its hiding place beside the water meter. It had gone. For a moment I was relieved, it meant he'd managed to climb up here, it meant he was still alive, they hadn't caught him yet. Then I had a kind of bad premonition, I opened the door quickly, I went straight into the office and slammed my hand down on the light switch. The strip light crackled and flickered several times before coming on but I could see that the drawer had been forced open and I knew I wouldn't find the pistol.

I had no more time to think because I heard the gate creaking and footsteps quickly approaching on the gravel path. I closed the door with my foot, went back into the main hall, and turned on all the lights so that when Bruce and three other boys appeared on the terrace I was in a full, harsh, yellow light. They asked me if Mo was there. I shook my head. I was afraid, my heart was pounding like the drums, I still had the memory of the last time they'd come visiting.

Bruce stayed outside while the three came in looking for Mo. I could vaguely make out Bruce's silhouette in the half-light but I knew he could see me perfectly and hoped that in every feature of my face he could read my hatred and disgust. He didn't move, neither did I.

After they'd left I paced around, turning a thousand things over in my mind, picturing the best outcome and the worst, I lingered on and at the back of my throat there was an acrid taste of smoke. In the end I fell asleep.

I open the door of the little kitchen that leads to the terrace. Every morning my gaze would be lost in the green of the trees, the russet red of the huts and beyond them, the blue of the lagoon. In my mind I'd thread my way along the twists and turns of the footpaths and swim with the dolphins. Every morning this magnificent, unreal view of the Bay of Mamoudzou was enough to give me energy and I'd forget the dregs, forget the violence, forget the filth. But today all I can see is a shantytown, all I can hear is anger, all I can see is the sea violated by deaths and blood, and I long to delve down into those dregs, to turn this violence inside out, I long to dive into the filth to retrieve Mo.

I stay here, hoping for a sight of Mo again as I saw him that first day on the far side of the road, standing there, motionless, his cap pulled down on his head, one hand holding on to the strap of his rucksack, the other in his pocket. That was a few months ago, I'd just arrived on Mayotte as part of my year of voluntary work with a certain NGO. My mission was to open a center for the youth of Kaweni. I'd been told it was like an inner city housing project, with youngsters hanging around, dealing on the black market, steeped in boredom, with no prospects, no jobs, drugs galore. A building had already been found, what was lacking was ideas. I was twenty-seven and just two of us had volunteered to come here. Mayotte is still part of France and no one was interested in that. The others wanted to go to Haiti, Sri Lanka, Bangladesh, Indonesia, Madagascar, Ethiopia. They wanted the "authentic" poverty, centuries-old destitution established like a deeply rooted canker, of "really hot countries," places where storms and wars are endemic, where earthquakes follow droughts. The favorite destination that looks great on your CV was still Gaza, and I mean the real Gaza, in Palestine, but that was reserved for the most experienced volunteers.

As for me, I just wanted to get away, so I signed up for Mayotte.

When Chebani, a member of the Mamoudzou fire brigade, who was also a volunteer with the same NGO as me, gave me a tour of Kaweni before showing me our building, I remember thinking, *But this is a shantytown.* As if he'd heard my thought, he turned to me and said *You weren't expecting this, were you?* I walked along behind him and we passed a baby who was whining like a little dog. Its left arm was burned, covered in blackened scabs and pink blisters here and there. It wasn't crying, or yelling, but was just sitting on the ground whining like a little wounded animal. A woman wrapped in a length of red-and-brown cloth emerged from a hut still talking animatedly to someone inside. She didn't pick up the child in her arms but sat down on the low wall beside it. The baby buried its head between the legs swathed in brown-and-red fabric and continued whimpering. I then made the stupidest remark of my life, *But, for heaven's sake, we're in France here!* and Chebani laughed until tears came into his eyes. Farther up he showed me a group of young people sitting under a breadfruit tree and behind them there was a wall on which GAZA had been graffitied in green. I took a photo of it and sent it to some friends in Paris. Ha, ha, very funny!

With two members of the local mission, Roukia and Toyba, two Mahorian women of about twenty, who'd lived on Réunion for a long time, we decided to make this clubhouse a place where young people could come and read, watch films, listen to music and play board games. We had no internet connection but we had this open, attractive pale yellow house, surrounded by fuchsia bougainvillea, we had a whole range of music, pop, rap, trap, R&B, classic hits, film screenings on Saturday evenings, domino tournaments and other games, and educational activities to help the young people escape from their "boredom." Maybe later we'd arrange literacy classes for anyone interested. Such were, more or less, the contents of the first report I sent to the Paris office.

It took us a good two weeks to move everything in, books, a good hi-fi system, an overhead projector, and several young people came to have a look. I was pleased, I'd learned several words in Shimaore, the local language, *kwezi, wawe ouhiriori bani, jeje bweni, marahaba, ewa,* "Good day, what's your name, good day *Madame,* thank you, yes," and my accent made them laugh but they never argued with me. Chebani told me to watch my step with "the little scumbags" but I didn't want to listen to other people, their cynicism, their views on every-thing, their judgment. I wanted to do things differently, not be the clichéd embodiment of the embattled, embittered humanitarian.

The newly elected member of parliament, a little man with a friendly, smiling face, opened the clubhouse one Thursday evening. He gave a speech to some fifty guests and very few young people. There were two TV cameras and women sing-ing merrily in Shimaore while banging on two pieces of wood. This reminded me of the claves, the hardwood sticks played in my youth when I was studying music at the Conservatoire. I was happy, convinced that I'd be doing good work here. The following day I'd arranged a film screening in the open air, with the overhead projector displaying the film on a big white sheet. I chose *Goldfinger* and the courtyard, the street, and the hillside were packed with people, dogs, and goats.

For a time the "Young People Forward" club was a roar-ing success. I received regular visits from the newly elected member who strolled about in the courtyard, his hands clasped behind his back as if all of this, the house, the garden, the hill, and all the huts one could see, belonged to him.

I steered clear of talk about the illegal immigrants, the burglaries, the lack of security. I lived in Combani, at the center of the island, in a little flat above a wrought-iron crafts-man's workshop. This was the countryside, where there were vast trees with grooved trunks that produced fruits that had a prehistoric look about them: enormous and twisted. Behind the house there was a large vegetable plot and in front of the house women sold their vegetables and slept beside them, on boards. I'd bought a motorbike and often rode around the island. On Saturday nights I'd go out with a group of friends whom I'd got to know around the place, among them midwives, nurses, young entrepreneurs, teachers, all young like me and white like me, with theories spilling out of their mouths and not an ounce of courage in their hands. To remake the world by grilling chicken on beaches, going clubbing, having a quick fuck, enjoying midnight swims, waking at noon to the sound of the muezzin, and diving in the most beautiful lagoon in the world, making the most of it, knowing that this was only a phase of our careers. Quite soon, in a year, two years, three at the very most, we'd be returning home, our pockets bulging with our bonuses, our hands still clasped behind our backs, and great theories still spilling out of our mouths.

But one day I saw Mo. Sometimes all it takes is a moment of truth for everything to tip over. He was standing on the other side of the dusty road, watching me opening boxes of books the club had just received. I'd never seen him before. I was sure of it because there was something about Mo, something that set him apart from the other local boys who always strolled around in twos and threes, I don't know how to explain it properly. It was as if he was there but in the blink of an eye he could vanish.

I stood up: would he like to help me bring in the books? For a moment he stayed there, leaning against the scrub-covered hillside the color of earth, and I remember shading my eyes with my hand, wondering if I'd been dreaming. But no, he detached himself from the slope and came over. He was tall and very thin. He kept his rucksack on his back and his cap on his head and began opening the boxes and carrying in the books. I noticed the tail end of a scar on his face, but as he kept his cap on I didn't see any more of it. He didn't say a word, but worked in silence with an economy of movement. Afterward we folded up the cardboard boxes and that was when I heard his voice for the first time. He asked me, in perfect French and in a husky voice, as if he'd not spoken for a long time *Could I keep one of these boxes please?*

I don't know why this voice broke my heart, I'm not ashamed to say this. I nodded vigorously, adding *Of course, of course, take as many as you want.* He thanked me and went away.

Mo came back a few times, always a little after the lunch hour when Gaza empties of its inhabitants and it's too hot to hang around. He'd help me if there was something to be done but often I let him be and he'd sit down with his book, always the same one, *The Boy and the River*, one hand on his brown rucksack, his cap always pulled well down on his head. Around four o'clock he'd turn down the corner of a page, stand up, come and find me wherever I was, offer me his hand, and say thank you in his voice that was still hoarse. Once or twice I tried to engage him in conversation, but he always kept his head down and his hands clung to the straps of his rucksack. I abandoned the attempt, mindful of what we'd been told at head office in Paris: always listen, but don't interfere.

At any rate the days passed quickly in a mixture of heat,

dust and noise. The adolescents themselves, the ones whom the administration referred to as "unaccompanied minors," kept their distance. When I came to work in the morning I'd see some of them at the entrance to the neighborhood, under the canopy of a grocer's shop or a little farther off beneath a more solid shelter. They'd watch me passing by with impassive faces, their bodies leaning forward, they were high, and I knew they'd been sleeping or been trying to sleep there. Sometimes, at the end of the morning, I'd see them again, the same ones or almost the same, sitting there, heads resting on chests, knocked out by joints and the heat.

One day the elected member invited me to a *mourengué*. He told me it was an ancestral style of fighting and I don't know why I assumed it was a variant of the martial art *capoeira*. He seemed pleased with the work of the club, telling me there had been a fall in delinquency, that people were less afraid to walk through Gaza, and, by the way, that this neighborhood should no longer be referred to as Gaza but could resume its proper name, Kaweni.

The drummers with their *gomas*, the local drums, were already there, as well as a sound system playing strong, rhythmic, traditional music. Night had fallen but it was still hot. A man stepped forwards with a whistle around his neck and the drumming began. Then two boys joined him, stripped to the waist, and when the signal was given they hurled themselves at one another, flinging out their arms and legs without any real technique. The one who fell to the ground first lost the round, and walked sheepishly back into the crowd, while the other did a few dance steps, to the rhythm of the *gomas* and even the strains of the referee's whistle. There were several rounds like that. The crowd laughed wholeheartedly, was quick to applaud and sometimes the fighters danced together, it was joyous, amusing, festive. Then this young man appeared. I'd never seen him before but the crowd began yelling, more in earnest than before, more solemnly almost, and the yelling drowned out the drumming of the *gomas*. There was a little boy beside me and I asked him *Who's he?* Eyes shining, he replied *That's Bruce, the Don of Gaza, he wins all the mourengués.* The winner of the previous bout, a sturdy young man, came dancing forward. His eyes were shut as if he were in a trance. Bruce went up to him. There was a group of youngsters behind him, I recognized a few, having seen them during the open-air film screenings. The atmosphere was no longer joyous but tense, uneasy. The referee blew his whistle and the fight began. Bruce was very strong, he dealt blows both with his head and his fists, his aim was good, he made good use of his energy and strength. His adversary held his own but his face was bleeding as the blows rained down on him. Suddenly Bruce kicked out and struck the other one in the belly. The thickset fighter fell to the ground. Unlike the other winners, Bruce didn't begin dancing but went over to his opponent on the ground and made as if to punch him in the face. The thickset young man brought his knees up to his chest and went into the fetal position. The crowd fell silent, only the *gomas* went on drumming and all of a sudden I had the impression that I was in a quite different space, a place of black magic, one with rules I didn't understand. Bruce stood up, raised his arm in the air and the crowd gave a joyous yell.

I slowly backed away as the crowd went up to the winner. I felt oppressed, ill at ease. Suddenly, from the shadows beneath a tree Mo emerged. I gave a start, like an idiot. Holding out his hand to me, he said *Bonsoir*, but I was scared, I didn't shake his hand I backed away from him and then quite frankly ran all the way back to the clubhouse. I got onto my motorbike and fled like a thief. I rode all the way home without stopping and the cooler the air became in the nocturnal shade of the great trees out in the country, the more ashamed I felt. The boy was barely fifteen.

I spent the weekend at home, ignoring calls from my friends to go and swim, dive, or dine. I couldn't stop thinking about the way Mo had emerged from beneath the tree and about his notably polite greeting. Had he wanted to ask me something? And what had I done? I'd turned and run as if I'd seen the devil.

It had been arranged that I'd spend a week at Kani-Kéli in the south of the island, to set up another youth club along the same lines as our own. On Monday I called in at the clubhouse in Gaza and waited for Chebani to come and bring me a car to drive to Kani-Kéli. He himself would take my motorbike. He arrived at ten o'clock at the wheel of an old gray Renault Clio, he said to me *I guess you've got your driver's license* and without waiting for my reply, roared with laughter and jumped astride the bike.

Maybe I'd had this idea since Friday night when I'd walked

away from Mo there in the darkness, maybe one regret led to another but when I saw him on a corner, sitting on the steps of one of the houses in the neighborhood, I opened the door of the Clio that I was driving cautiously through Gaza's narrow streets and said to him *Would you like to come for a ride?* He stayed sitting there and I pressed him *Go on! Come along!*

He stood up, tightened the strap on his rucksack a little, tugged on the peak of his cap so it came down a bit farther over his face, and got into the car. He smelled of sweat and old clothes, his legs were the color of ash. He put his rucksack at his feet and fastened his seat belt, and I started the car.

Ten minutes later, we'd barely reached Mamoudzou, and Mo was asleep, softly snoring like an exhausted child.

Moïse

When I got into that car there was the hum of the air conditioning, the softness of the seat behind my back, the carpet I could run my feet over. Stéphane said nothing, he drove carefully, in silence, with no music, it was pleasant. I could feel my body letting go, my eyelids growing heavy and I didn't even struggle against it.

When I woke up I was alone in the car. I got up with a start, first of all checking my rucksack and then my scar. I always do that when I wake up, I don't know why. I know it'll still be there but I can't stop myself from checking the puffy line that runs across my face. Maybe every morning I have the illusion that I've made a leap back in time to earlier days, returned to my past life, and that this scar was just a bad dream. Or maybe I'm scared of it getting bigger, growing longer, closing my eye for good, and traveling all around my head and body, as in that recurring nightmare when the mosquito netting over my bed becomes a snake, wrapping itself around me, stifling me.

The car was parked beside a house in the shade of a flame tree. I looked around, there was no one there. I waited for a moment, not knowing what to do, maybe Stéphane would come back at any minute? The garden was surrounded by a bamboo hedge. There were several shrubs in the yard, down at the far end, plants in pots here and there, and some brightly colored children's toys. Red, green, yellow.

I got out of the car cautiously, keeping one hand on the open door. The air was hot, but it wasn't the furnace of Gaza. I inhaled a breath and there wasn't a smell of anything. It was so good. I heard the sound of birds above me and further off as well, in the depths of the garden, on the other side of the bamboo hedge, behind me and more distantly, everywhere, in fact, the birds were calling.

I took off my cap, I let go of the car door, I looked up at the flame tree. The sky seen through its leaves and branches was like a blue, green and brown picture, a picture that stirred in the wind or maybe it was me swaying a little. I closed my eyes. I'd have liked to be able to fly, to view this miserable world from on high, very high, to be unreachable, unassailable, invincible, invisible. I'd have liked to be a birdman, no I'd have liked simply to be a bird chirruping here, there and everywhere. I imagined my bones and body shrinking, my pores opening to let green feathers sprout from them, the same green as my eye, I felt my scar disappearing, my eyes growing round and very mobile, my face extending, my mouth changing into a black, pointed, shining beak, my brain becoming the size of a pea, my memories floating away in smoke, my claws preparing for takeoff, my wings opening out and now I'm flying, I perch on the flame tree's thick sturdy branch. I'm both light and powerful. I sing. I light up the sun, I make the rain fall, I make wonders unfold.

When I opened my eyes, Stéphane was in front of me, staring at me. He pointed to the right side of my face and asked *Who did that to you?* His voice was hard, kind of high-pitched, different from his normal one and maybe I was tired of hiding, maybe it was the cutting edge of his voice, maybe because I was still a bird (and birds don't know how to lie), I said *It was Bruce.*

He took a deep breath and opened his mouth as if he was about to say something and I didn't want to hear any of his pity or his questions, but he simply asked me if I was hungry and, relieved, I said *Yes.*

We walked over to the restaurant and then Stéphane told me we were in Kani-Kéli. *Do you know it, Mo, have you been here before?*

I shrugged. I thought about how I'd begged Marie to bring me here to the south of the island and she'd refuse, saying *You're not ready for it yet!* Am I ready now? I don't know. How can I tell Stéphane that I came here as a baby in my mother's arms on board a *kwassa-kwassa* to Bandrakouni just a few miles from here and that since then everything has got mixed up in my head. I'd dreamed so much about that beach but now I was so close to it I no longer knew what I wanted, no longer knew what was good for me.

Stéphane could never understand things like that. I don't judge him, I've seen guys like him spending a few months in Gaza, I don't know what their aim is, I don't know if they really believe a few film screenings, a few soccer games, or some American pop music will be enough to make us forget the poverty, the filth, and the violence. They know a lot of things, those guys, they know the figures on poverty, they know the statistics on petty crime, they study graphs of violence, words like culture and leisure spring readily to their lips, but they never truly understand anything. Only a street kid can know the joy of finding an old toothbrush on the ground, washing it in the gully, and rubbing it with an old piece of soap, old soap, so hard and marked with black stripes that it's like a stone, but you rub away at it all the same and afterward you go into a corner because you don't want anyone to steal this brush from you and you clean your teeth with it, you turn the brush around in your mouth as if it were a lollipop and, the joy of that, only a kid who lives on the street can know that. There's no film screening or soccer match that can equal the fact of owning something, some object that belongs to you and you alone, even if it's only an old toothbrush.

I don't much like remembering that week at Kani-Kéli. It was as if I'd been made to act in a film where I played the part of an ordinary young boy with no problems. I was helping Stéphane to refurbish the little house that would soon be a home to a club like "Young People Forward." He told me to wash down and I washed down. He told me to scrape the paintwork and I scraped. He told me to paint and I painted. He told me to sweep and I swept. He told me to hold up the shelves while he fixed them to the wall and I held them up. When he was working on his computer I'd open my copy of *The Boy and the River* and reread it for the thousandth time but no matter. When people came I stayed in my corner cleaning, scraping, painting, washing, and reading and people ignored me. When Stéphane spoke to me I listened but I never really took in his words, they were like raindrops falling on my skin, falling, falling, and then there was a great pool of words at my feet. When he told me to rest I went into the garden to sit under the flame tree. He'd say to me, go and take a walk, get some air, go onto the beach, but I stayed under the flame tree, listening to the birds and imagining myself flying around the trunk and my wings beating so fast that all the colors of my feathers blended together. When Stéphane asked me why I always read the same book I shrugged because I didn't want to explain to him that this book was like a kind of talisman that protected me from the real world, that the words in this book which I knew by heart were like a prayer that I repeated over and over again and it may well be that no one heard me, maybe it served no purpose, but no matter. Opening this book was like opening my own life, that insignificant little life of mine on this island, and in it I made contact with Marie again and the house and it was the only way I'd found of not going mad, of not losing track of the little boy I'd once been.

I didn't speak much, I didn't think much, I did what he told me to do because that week I realized that was all I was good for. Bruce had trained me to be a good dog and that week I'd been a good dog, clean and well fed.

On Thursday morning Stéphane fastened a big map of Mayotte to the wall and stuck a red drawing pin in at the spot where we were, Kani-Kéli. I went up closer and just an inch away from it, a little lower down, I saw Bandrakouni. I stared at this name which was both mysterious and familiar. Suddenly, by magic, it began floating away from the map, first one letter, then another, BANDRAKOUNI and they came flying up to me like angry wasps, they were on my face, on my scar, I tried to drive them away but they became embedded in my skin and I started yelling . . .

I was lying flat on a mattress in the living room and the light outside was as white as a sheet. I had a pain in my right eye and my scar was throbbing. I put a hand over it, hoping to calm it down. Stéphane was there but he said nothing. I was relieved at not being alone, at not being on the hill at Gaza, at knowing Bruce was far away. I kept my hand over my face, I waited a little and then I told Stéphane I'd like to go onto the beach at Bandrakouni. He simply said *OK*.

I was convinced that nothing would ever appear beautiful to my eyes again, that nothing could awaken me from the lethargic state I'd been sunk in since Marie's death. Stéphane told me he'd drop me off at Bandrakouni for the time it took him to call on a friend. In the car, as it drove slowly along my gaze was drawn irresistibly to the sea unfurling its blue, emerald, green and opaline. To our left we could see Mount Choungui. In the meadows old freezers served as drinking troughs for the animals. At the roadsides men and women walked along with baskets on their heads and sticks or machetes in their hands. The sky was cloudless and as we traveled through this idyllic landscape, something made my heart swell. What was this sweet, beautiful country? What was this country that had forgotten me?

It's there Stéphane said, stopping the car at the side of the road. I got out, he drove off at once.

So it was there. I followed a shady path lined with shrubs where tiny butterflies darted about, as well as with tall trees, eucalyptus and mangoes. Their branches formed sinuous traceries over my head, I could hear the sea, I could hear the birds, at every step there was a crackle of dry leaves. It was there.

I came to a little bay in the shape of a crescent moon and now, beneath my feet, black sand, as black as my skin. Behind me, as if shielding the island and forming a ring around the bay, a number of baobab trees. Inside their trunks, as I'd been taught at school, there's always a hollow. I don't know what purpose it serves.

I walked up and down, made a tour of all the baobabs. At the base of one there were charred logs and a mound of gray ashes. People came here to grill meat, they came to swim, to eat, to enjoy themselves, they didn't come here like me with anguish in the pit of their stomachs and a longing to discover something or other in the hope that this beach might answer all the questions, fill all the empty spaces, shine light into all the shadows.

What should I do now? I stood still, listening to the sound of the delicate waves, the hissing noise that came from the rocks, the shrill birdcalls. I'd finally returned to where it had all begun but this was only a beach. Fifteen years ago my mother had landed at this very spot with other illegal immigrants but there was no trace of them today. The tides had washed away their footprints on the black sand, the wind had blown back their shouts across the open sea. I'd have liked to be able to say that I saw a sign, that I recognized a particular birdcall, that a wise and comforting phrase had been whispered in my ear, that I could read a mark on the trunk of one of the baobabs, that I felt less alone, all those magical things I'd imagined and cherished in my mind when I thought about this place. Bandrakouni.

The delicate, foam-fringed waves washed in and wove their collars of lace about my ankles. I went into the sea. My body stretched out in the water, I cupped my hands, I began kicking my legs in a scissors action, and the movements learned long ago came back to me. Breathe, thrust forward, breathe, thrust forward. I swam silently, not thinking about much, except the positioning of my arms and legs, and the way my head needed to break the surface to enable me to breathe. Maybe if I'd been stronger, more intelligent, I'd have swum to another shore and tried to live another life, differently, in another way. But when it comes to boys like me, who live in constant fear, who've had everything and suddenly have nothing, we go back, just like lambs to the slaughter.

When I returned to the shore at Bandrakouni I realized that I was about the same age as my mother had been when she landed on this beach of black sand surrounded by baobab trees. Had she been afraid then? In the dark during the crossing? Had I cried? Did she know that baobabs contain a hollow space inside them, one into which she could have slipped me? I'd have fallen asleep, then I'd have died there in that hollow and I'd have become a little bit of that tree, invincible, admirable. It's a glorious life being a baobab tree on a beach.

Bruce

You always thought you were different from the rest of us. There was something in you I could never put my finger on, get a grip on, rub out. Sometimes when I saw you sat there, unmoving as a stone, I had the urge to shake you, and say there was no point in your sitting there, boys like you and me were made to grapple with life, get stuck in and snuff it with no regrets. No mercy, Mo. No mercy. You're just like the rest of us, Mo. You're black, you're alone, you're trapped here, you're on the street.

I knew you spent your afternoons up there in that white fool's place, the one who looks like nothing on earth. His skin's so pale he looks as if he's dead already, he's as thin as a drumstick and does your head in with all his talk and his soccer games. Before every film he thinks he has to spout loads of stuff about the actor or the guy that made it or even tell the plot, is he a fucking fool or what?

I always thought you were watching TV up in the room there, but no, *you're reading*. That's all you do, sit there and read. But I let you carry on, I was keeping you in reserve, the way I keep all my homeboys in reserve. I told myself one day you'd be useful to me for something. I knew you were cunning, the djinn doesn't choose fools and weaklings, Mo, believe me. I knew perfectly well you hadn't gone out of your mind, I knew you hadn't gone nuts, I knew I needed to be wary of you. But you stayed quiet, you came when I called, you did what I told you, and maybe I should have kept a closer watch on you.

You chose your moment, didn't you. I was too easy that weekend, I'd beaten that dumb bastard Abdallah in the *mourengué*. He was the champion over at M'tsapété and he thought he was cunning and strong enough to come and challenge me on my own turf. MY OWN TURF? You saw him there on the ground crying for his mother. That weekend we had good drinks, good smokes, good dancing, on Saturday night we went to Ninga disco and couldn't get in like we usually did. It was the bouncer, that fucking African fool who came here on a *kwassa-kwassa* like a half-starved wretch, but who now thinks he's an American in his dark suit. I had enough money to have fuck and my prick was itching for it, I'd had enough of bleating goats, I was the king for fuck's sake. I gave cash to La Teigne, Rico, and Nasse, who'd come back from Anjouan on a *kwassa-kwassa*, and they all had a fuck in the bushes, front and back, and afterward we washed our pricks in Mamoudzou Harbor. I felt good. Same thing on Sunday. I had enough cash to buy a whole box of chicken and Nasse grilled it all properly, chili pepper, cassava, the whole of Gaza smelled of home-cooked kebabs, the blue smoke attracted all the kids, it was a feast. Bruce was king, it was all too good. You know very well, you ate your share the same as everyone else.

Then on Monday, what do I hear, you've gone off with the

white man in a gray car. Like, he opened the door and you got in, he didn't even force you. He's not a cop you know.

You chose your moment didn't you. Didn't you know how things go on my turf, ON MY TURF? How long've you been here, hey? A year at least, didn't you know you need my permission to leave Gaza?

Monday, Tuesday, Wednesday still no show. Nasse told me you were in Kani-Kéli with a white man, what the fuck were you up to in Kani-Kéli, for fuck's sake? I shouldn't't've cared but I couldn't let it go. When I thought about what you were doing with the *muzungu* it drove me nuts, were you his bitch? His favorite little black *sousou*? All my homies were hurting my head, La Teigne, Rico, Nasse, the youths, all looked at me the way you never did, waiting for what I'd decide, waiting with open beaks.

And I could see they thought I was stressing too much about you. A king can't give in to that kind of weakness. A king can't allow things like that to happen on his turf. I had to take back control.

On Thursday at nightfall I made a tour of the streets of Gaza, my homies handed over what the youths had collected, and told me they'd run out of spliffs, smokes, spice. Some of them were so withdrawn they were smoking mangrove leaves. *Tss.* I didn't like that. Their eyes were tiny and dry, their mouths were puckered and they were all calling out *Bruce Bruce* leaping around me like starving dogs. I had all my stock brought down, there wasn't much left but that calmed the crowd a bit. Stuff needed to happen, I wanted fire, noise, Gaza had been too quiet since the election. That night I decided to go pay a visit to the clubhouse. I took La Teigne and Rico with me.

What a clown. He'd fixed it with a rotten chain and two padlocks. He thought he was safe, that the politician would protect him with his sweet talk but I'm the one here who decides who's safe and who isn't. We took it apart with a crowbar, making no noise, and spent two hours moving everything, all the equipment, without anyone bothering us. The TV, the overhead projector, the hi-fi, the computer, the DVDs, the CDs. We got the books out and I was going to set fire to them but I pissed on them instead. Rico and La Teigne took out their pricks and we gave it all a good watering.

On Friday the political representative came for prayers in his posh metallic gray Nissan and I told him the white man had gone off with one of my friends. He stared at me as if I was speaking Chinese. I went up to him, he smelled of perfume and soap, he'd put on his white tunic, I had a sudden vision of my father in front of me but it didn't last long. As I spoke he caught a whiff of my spliff-smoker's breath, and blinked. I said *They're homos.* He backed away, raising his hands level with his chest and said *I don't want any of that here.* I smiled and murmured, *I'll take care of it boss.* Politicians like it when you call them *boss.* That's how slaves addressed their masters, did you know that, Mo? With a nod he laid his hand on my shoulder and went on his way dressed in his fine white tunic, hoisting it up a little because he didn't want the mud of Gaza to soil the hem.

On Saturday we sold everything, it was all good gear from

France, no *made in China*, and in Gaza that evening there was chicken, Coke, grass, cigarettes, spice, beer, and more besides. After that we hung out near the Ninga, and waited until the *sousous* were leaving and flashed our cash. I found one, a girl from Madagascar with her hair tied up on her head who wanted to talk at first. She told me about her shitty life, how she came to Mayotte with a *muzungu*, how he dumped her three days later, just three days later, she kept saying, and she had a child and nothing to buy milk with and no papers and was forced to become a *sousou*. I let her talk because she was really beautiful and spoke softly and prettily. I was good, everything was good, out there Gaza was having a good time drinking and smoking, and I was fucking a beautiful, gentle girl, for once I was careful with her hair, I didn't want her ponytail to come undone, it looked pretty like that, I was careful with her face, but all of a sudden, as I was fucking her, I thought of you and what you were doing with that *muzungu* with a dead man's skin and it drove me nuts. I stopped being gentle, I stopped being careful with the whore and grabbed her hair with both hands and hammered her with all my rage.

Stéphane

They all keep telling you about it, yet mysteriously you still think you're safe. They tell you how that pretty girl you've seen several times at parties was attacked on a beach and because she wouldn't let go of her camera the thieves hit her with a coconut to knock her out. Now half her pretty face is paralyzed. They tell you about the places in the woods where illegal immigrants have been living for dozens of years. You read articles about violent sexual assaults committed by young boys under the influence of this new drug called "spice" and later when you're talking to your friends about what you've read, they can even give you the first name of the guy who imported it into Mayotte and you say *Fuck that's scary* but it doesn't get to you where it ought to get to you. They tell you how during the holidays the *muzungus* are increasingly renting their houses to tourists for a handful of euros so they also act as caretakers. They point out the big dogs abandoned by departing *muzungus*, because where they're going they'll have no need of three German shepherds to guard their homes. They ask you if you've been on that small island of white sand and you tell them about that wonderful day you spent there diving in the most beautiful lagoon in the world, yes, now you're sure of it, it's the most beautiful lagoon in the whole world, since you've seen this emerald and opaline domain with your own eyes and, even if you know that hundreds of people drown there, you still say *It's the most beautiful lagoon in the world.* They whisper that half the inhabitants of Mayotte are illegal immigrants, that all the infrastructure on the island has been designed for a population of two hundred thousand but that unofficially there must be almost four hundred thousand people here and you say *But that's not possible, it'll explode* and this remark of yours has been uttered thousands of times already. They say to you *Look, he's a Mahorian, he's from Grand Comore, he's from Anjouan, he's from Madagascar* but the truth is they all look the same to you. They suggest you take a trip along the minor roads that run across the island and you're amazed at all the vegetable plots and houses on the hills. They tell you it's the illegal immigrants from Anjouan who till the fields and the *muzungus* who live in the houses on hilltops. They tell you that if this goes on, and the French state does nothing, the Mahorians themselves are going to take their fate into their own hands and kick out all the illegal immigrants and delinquents. So you have a vision of hundreds of blacks coming down into the street with machetes and you no longer know whether it's an image from Rwanda or Zimbabwe or the Congo and you say *That'll never happen in a* département *of the French state.*

Here's what you've witnessed yourself, one day, when you're waiting to cross the road to buy a new telephone card: two motorbikes collide. Three people fall to the ground in front of you. On the sidewalk side a man with gray hair, a checked shirt, black trousers, not wearing a helmet. On the street side a man in a helmet wearing green Bermuda shorts (the kind that have big pockets, inside which are average sized pockets, inside which there are little pockets) and a white T-shirt; behind him, fallen in almost exactly the same position, a little girl in a dress with pink flowers on it and cornrow braids running along the top of her head which can be seen because she's not wearing a helmet. You stop in your tracks at the metallic clatter the bikes make as they crash and, very quickly, you see the helmeted man get up, leap onto his bike and ride off, revving his engine noisily. The little girl remains motionless on the ground. You see, but you don't really get it. The emergency services arrive and the little girl is carried into the first aid vehicle. The man with gray hair is very upset and says *He abandoned her! He abandoned her, just like that.* When he says *Just like that,* he points to the ground with his hand and you see that his forearm's all bloody. The flesh is pink, the blood's red, the dangling skin's black and you say to yourself that this is the first time you've seen a black man bleeding.

The next day, when you see Chebani you ask for news of that little girl and he tells you she's been taken to the hospital. You ask if the little girl had any papers. Chebani stares at you as if you were an extraterrestrial. *Of course she has no papers, she didn't even know her age. And that guy who abandoned her didn't have any papers either.* He laughs and slaps you on the back and says *Caribou, welcome to Mayotte.*

They tell you to be careful and give you the example of the firemen's barracks on the other side of the main street which was broken into that night. They say to you *All that gear in the clubhouse it's like dangling chunks of meat in front of lions.* They repeat *You don't know these youngsters*, they keep drumming into you *Don't use your phone in the street, don't go to the cash machine alone, don't carry a shoulder bag.* But you carry on with your life, believing you'll be safe because you've been safe for the first twenty-five years of it and that's all you've ever known.

But then your life's turned upside down when you come back from a week in the south where you've been working from dawn to dusk, where you got the impression, no, it wasn't just an impression, it was the certainty that you'd not only been bringing a building back to life but also a young boy who didn't talk during the daytime but who said things in his sleep at night and you listened so as to stitch together his words and piece together his story and when he stopped wearing his cap you had the feeling of knowing how it feels, well, to be a good man.

All those books on the ground with buckled pages, you didn't need to sniff them to know they'd been pissed on. You know the clubhouse has been wrecked and burglarized but you can't manage to tear your eyes away from all these books on the ground and you don't know why it makes you think of little mutilated bodies that you're going to have to put into a pile and burn.

Your life's turned upside down when they come back to the

clubhouse, rough you up and call you a pedophile, a homo. As they bear down on you, you'd like to be a solid and inviolable wall, but no, you retreat, you stammer, you have no strength in your arms. You stumble around on the books making a sound like dead leaves. You're afraid, your stomach rises into your throat, it's the first time you've ever been attacked and it's not at all how you'd pictured it. You saw yourself facing up to it, standing firm, you saw yourself as taller, stronger, braver. Two boys hold you down on the ground with their hands and knees. They twist your arm a bit and lean hard on your stomach. You remember them smelling of iron and smoke. The two others surround Mo and he doesn't protest, doesn't weep, doesn't even look at you. They take him away with them in the harsh light of this Monday morning and the ones who were holding you down go running off as well.

You stay on the ground for a long time, you're scared but a great feeling of relief comes over you. Their grudge wasn't really with you. You stand up and go out into the courtyard to be sick.

The same evening your friends come to see you and comfort you and you tell them your story the way they once told you stories and now they say *Fuck that's scary* and this time it gets to you in the belly and it touches a part of you that's as raw and red as the blood of the man in the checked shirt, a part of you that's just been born, and is as tender as everything that's just been born and you feel a pain in your stomach, you weep. You go out with them every evening, from now on you're never alone and you can't stop telling the story of what happened to you. One evening a friend of one of your friends offers you a pistol for self-defense and you take it. Now, and only now, do you understand.

Moïse

I'm thinking about that day still, I have to keep thinking about it, because if it hadn't been for that day, I'd never have committed murder, I'd never have listened to Stéphane when he was banging on about the pistol he kept in his desk, I wouldn't have had this black hole inside me that everything now falls into with a dull sound never to surface again. In this square cell where at times a draft of air comes in and strangely cools my brow, in this room where I seem to hear breathing and sighs that are not my own, I know, I feel strangely at peace. I now know that what happened that day and that night, and on all those days and nights that have brought me here, is much greater than my pain, my sorrow, my regret.

I'm fifteen years old, my name's Moïse, I was born on the other side of the water. My mother was afraid of me, my mother pitied me and herself. She wondered what she'd done to God and all the djinns to have a child with one dark eye and one green one. My mother handed me over, like an old parcel, to the first person who came along but I know now that it wasn't her fault, I know now you need money to go on a *kwassa-kwassa*, you need courage to go on board these fragile boats. I know now what it looks like, that beach at Bandrakouni, with its baobab trees that resemble ramparts, I know you need to feel something else in your bowels apart from just pity and fear. I know you need a little love.

When they came to fetch me, I didn't protest. They have a way, Bruce's homies, of walking along in a semicircle around you as if they were keeping you company, as if you were one of their own and I don't suppose anyone who saw us in the filthy alleyways of Gaza that morning paid us any attention. No one pays any attention to five bad boys.

We passed that same garage with the same light bulb in the ceiling, the one that smelled of gasoline and metal and that once more set my teeth on edge.

A dense blue pool shining in the sun lay stagnant at the bottom of the gully. Bruce was upstream under the shade of the breadfruit tree. He sat on a black rock watching us approach. He was smiling, his white teeth gleaming. I wasn't afraid, not yet. I knew he'd be furious that I'd gone off without telling him. I remembered one of the youths returning to Gaza because his mother, who had six other babies, couldn't feed him. Bruce had tied him to a tree and for an hour every member of the gang walked past him and hit him on his thighs or his arms with a thin branch still in leaf. When the leaves had fallen off, someone went and picked another branch. I did it too, with a single blow, *thwack*, without looking him in the eye. Then he was sent back to beg from the *muzungus* coming off the ferry and for several months his scarred thighs and arms were a great success.

I told myself that maybe he had something like that in store for me, even if, for my part, I never actually brought anything in for him. Me, Scarface Mo, the nutjob, the mute, whom he'd branded already. Maybe he'd tie me up for a whole day and command his homies to pick branches with no leaves, ones that prick and scratch? As I walked up toward the breadfruit tree that morning that was my way of *preparing for the worst*.

Bruce beckoned me to come up to him, sent my cap flying with a blow of his hand and brought his face close to mine. He smelled of bitter, dense spice smoke, his breath was heavy but his teeth were milky white.

He drew his index finger lightly along my scar and I didn't move. And said *That's soft.*

Then he crooked that same index finger and this time drew his nail along my scar as if he meant to scratch it. I started shaking. Making his voice shrill he asked *Had a good time in Kani-Kéli with your darlin' did you?*

The others around him roared with delight, their coarse laughter erupting as if from the throat of one man and from the depths of my memory, I don't know why, the words came to me from that book I so love, "Then all the beasts stirred. It was the awakening."

I'm no longer afraid, now. Bruce is dead, I killed him this morning in the woods, he won't come back.

In Bruce's *banga* my hands and feet were bound with a rope.

On the TV screen men and women were fucking.

I was getting a hard-on in my shorts and I was so ashamed. The homies pointed at my prick and laughed.

On the TV screen men were having dogs and dogs having women.

The music went *rap rap nigga nigga fuck fuck*.

My stomach was churning.

On the TV screen, men were fucking men who were fucking women who were fucking dogs.

In the *banga* the homeboys laughed then moved fast.

Around me a stink of bitter sweat.

I was able to bring my legs up to my chest and the feeling of my own knees against me was very comforting.

They crushed pills, piled up mangrove leaves, emptied cigarettes, drank beer in front of me.

On the TV there were rap tracks *fuck fuck fuck* went the rappers in thick, heavy voices and women flaunted and shook their asses as though they had a life of their own.

I don't know how much time it went on for.

Bruce came in and there was this silence, even the TV went quiet or maybe I've imagined it. He said *Come here my darlin'*. I felt a hot liquid wetting my thighs. Someone said *He's pissed himself* but Bruce repeated *Come here my darlin'*.

But all that's nothing compared to the time that slowly passes by moment by moment and what you hear and see. You hear your dog and picture him breaking down the door and biting Bruce just as he's thrusting his prick into your flesh. You imagine Bruce yelling not because he's king of Gaza and is taking possession of you the way he takes possession of every speck of dust here, but because a dog has just leapt at his throat, gripping it right around the Adam's apple and won't let go, no, he won't let go, Bosco.

You hear horses and you know there are no horses but you hear the *clip clop clip clop* coming closer and soon a stampede will crush the *banga* and everything in it.

You see a slipper and it's so white you wonder whether it isn't brand new and you dream up a whole story about this new white slipper that's so perfect, while La Teigne or Nasse or Rico or whoever are thrusting other things into your flesh.

You see a panga propped against the door and in your head you list all the names for this tool, beginning with *coupe-coupe*, *chombo*, machete, billhook, big knife, Chinese knife, cutlass and this brings you back to the throat that your dog has now ripped out and drops at your feet as an offering.

You tell yourself that, like in the book, like Pascalet and Gatzo, you have "*racals*" at your back, those fierce animals that linger in lonely places, prowling through the night and pounce on you with a prodigious spring, the well-known spring of the *racal* which surpasses that of the tiger.

While Bruce smokes and drinks and watches you having things thrust into your flesh, with his yellowed *racal*'s eyes, with a smile that never leaves his lips, you think about the word "prodigious" and you try to find something in your life that could be "prodigious."

I can't find anything.

I think about Marie and about the woman next door who didn't like going out during the day, I think about the beach at Bandrakouni and I travel through time, it's a time that lasts so long when boys of your own age are raping you, boys who know how to laugh and smile, who eat and shit like you, like me. And they could have lived in a place called Tahiti, a place called Poitiers, a place called Montreal and they'd certainly have been different. I travel back through time and get to that beach where a *kwassa-kwassa* is disembarking its sick passengers, its burn victims, its cursed child. I whisper in my mother's ear and she slips me inside a baobab tree and I don't weep as I'm doing here, now that everyone has left, night has fallen and the stink of shit and sweat and spunk and vomit has overwhelmed the *banga*, I don't weep because I'm safe in the hollow of a baobab tree.

When I crawl outside the sky's inscribed with strange indecipherable words, words that the stars have drawn, and the moon is moving from right to left like a laser and I know I've entered another world, another dimension and never again will I be as I was before.

Bruce

I know I'm a rude boy. Even here, in this dim gray place, where it's as if night will fall at any moment, I can still feel the anger and disgust and there's always this odd taste in my mouth like my teeth are rotting. I want to leave now, I've seen enough, I want to get back to the dust and smell of Gaza. One more time I want to see the fear and admiration in everyone's eyes when I walk into Gaza. *Bruce is here Bruce, Bruce* and the music of it all following me in the streets, down into the gully, as I stopped to talk to the guys in the workshop, went up to my *banga*, or passed the old waterfall, that music gave me wings and I strode along as Bruce, head held high, handing out good marks and bad, spliffs and slaps, beers and kicks, and I told myself I was truly like Batman and I'd really like to rename Gaza Gotham City, that would've had some style.

I know I'm a rude boy, I know I could've spared you, especially when you pissed yourself, but that wasn't happening, Mo, that's not how you get to be king of the ghetto. Have you ever heard about Mr. T? Back in the day his word was law in the neighborhood. His name was Kaphet but soon as he started wearing thick gold chains around his neck, he got people calling him Mr. T. Word was he'd killed *muzungus* with his bare hands, that he was against France and the French, he always used to say *It's the Comoros Islands here, not France* and he had a green-and-white flag painted on the wall of his house. They said he knew all the police on the island, the prefect, the elected members and that even the *cadis*, the Muslim judges, were afraid of him. He tattooed himself with needles he used to heat in the flame of a paraffin stove. He couldn't read or write, he didn't smoke, this motherfucker, and he didn't drink, either, but every evening he'd tattoo designs on himself by hand which he did at an amazing speed, you'd have to see him to believe it. He'd inhale with his mouth almost closed as he made the needle turn red in the blue flame.

But it's not enough to have a reputation and the tales they tell about you. I didn't know him when he was young and scared everyone. I only knew him when he went around patting little girls and boys on the head and handing out milk to their *mamans* without asking for anything back. They used to say to me *He's the Daddy of Kaweni*, and I wanted to laugh. Mr. T. used to get young people together, and talked about building them *bangas*, talked about cleaning up the neighborhood, going back to school. He got them to write up on the wall, "Education to stop violence." But Mr. T. let things slide. The kids did as they liked, there were raids, they arrested illegal immigrants in their houses. The law came back into the neighborhood as if it was their turf! Imagine that! But Mr. T. went on preaching about dialogue, he had no reputation anymore, just his tattoos and his jewelry. And do you know what happened to Mr. T.? He was beaten up in his own home and strangled with his own chain from around his neck. No one came to weep for him. He'd become just another guy, he didn't scare people anymore.

I didn't want to end up like that. You get me, Mo, everyone watches you when you're the Don. Everyone watches you to see if you're going soft, if you're smiling too much, if you're starting to shuffle along, to drink too much, if you're getting out of touch, and there's always some homeboy close to you who thinks he can take your place. It could be Rico, Nasse, or La Teigne. And them youths, you know what they've got in their heads? *When I grow up I'll be like Bruce* that's what they've got in their heads, those ragamuffins.

There was this talk that I was protecting you, that I never sent you out to beg from the *muzungus*, or do burglaries, that I was just letting you hang out in Gaza. I'd heard this talk for some time, but I ignored it. I told myself that a day would come when you'd be useful to me, your green eye, your scar, your brown rucksack. I don't know why I'd got that kind of idea in my head, maybe to begin with I liked you.

When you went off to Kani-Kéli for a week without asking my permission I didn't want them to think I'd become weak and that people could do what they liked in my neighborhood and I thought again about Mr. T. going around patting children's heads and handing out cans of milk with a smile. I thought about the way he died, beaten up in his own home, strangled with his own neck chain.

So you get me, Mo, I had to punish you and it had to stick in everyone's memory, so my homeboys would go tell their friends about it and they'd tell their friends and the story would spread across Gaza, now, tomorrow, so that once more and for all time they'd all be afraid of me. I didn't want to end up like Mr. T.

I showed them what to do, then I watched. I said *Go ahead* they went ahead. I said *Stop* they stopped. I said *Untie him* they untied. I said *Wash him* they washed. I said *Dress him* they dressed. I said *Give him a drink* they gave you a drink. I said *Get the fuck out of here* and everyone did.

It's a fine victory. Just me and my homies, my feet and theirs tramping through the dry leaves from the tropical almond trees, people backing away in front of us, children following us at a safe distance, skipping along. I'm untouchable. I've become a star. For days and days until the night of the *mourengué*, I hear the same music in my ears and think it'll never stop. I'll be the king forever.

And you went nuts. You started talking to yourself, and pointing your finger at the sky, and went back to your friend Stéphane. Nutjob Mo, that's what they started calling you. Some people told me to get rid of you but I wanted you to be there for all to see. I wanted everyone to know what's in store for anyone who betrays Bruce.

I'd've done better to think of my father and remember all he told me about the djinn. I should have known I could never escape the djinn's green eye.

Moïse

There were times when the trees would suddenly line up in rows in front of me, the earth swallowed up all the filth, the pathways became straight and luminous and the birds came down from the trees and stood to attention.

There were times when the green from the leaves came flowing down *plop plop* and I began running away, but then the blue from the sky started dripping down as well *plop plop* and the green and the blue came spilling down on me like thick tar and it was all so heavy that I remained at a standstill, smothered under its weight.

There were times when teeth and hair sprouted on the men working at the tinsmith's workshop and as I walked by they began to bark.

There were times when Bosco appeared at my side, much bigger, much stronger. I'd talk to him and he'd nod his head.

There were times when everything was as before, the smell, the heat, the noise, the dust and I remembered that Bosco was dead and I'd see Bruce and his homies and remember what they'd done to me in the *banga* and I wanted to die.

One day I found myself beside the clubhouse. It was a day with no sky. There were two boys I didn't know and I stayed outside looking up at the dark space above my head. Then Stéphane appeared, waving his arms and gave me back my rucksack. *You'd left it in the car* he said. Then he began talking nonstop. I followed him into the clubhouse where there was a strong smell of bleach. I sat down on the ground and maybe I had a nap, maybe I had something to eat, but I know I said nothing. Maybe it was on that day or some other day that Stéphane told me about his gun. Maybe it was on that day when the sky had disappeared and the trees were following me that he told me he'd soon be going back to France and the clubhouse was going to close down and he seemed both pleased and sad and, as the trees behind him drew closer to listen, he said *I'm so sorry, Mo.*

Time passes, night follows day and none of it matters.

That evening, when I heard the drums, I was in the woods and Bosco had reappeared again. Now Bosco was very big, he had the same close-cropped coat with dark patches as before but people were afraid of him, I could see how they stepped aside as I walked along.

The *mourengué* had started and Rico had beaten a boy I didn't know. He was dancing and Bosco began to growl. Then La Teigne came up and was beaten by Rico. Bosco squeezed up against me, I could feel his well-fleshed side pressing against me, his muscles tensing and relaxing as he breathed. The crowd was getting bigger. Then Bruce came into the arena and the drums beat faster. Stronger, faster, and when the whistle blew he toppled Rico with a kick and the crowd surged like a great wave, swelling, rising up, and then falling back at the feet of Bruce, the king. Bosco said to me *Go on Moïse* because my dog knew my name and his voice was firm, his serious, powerful, magic dog's voice rang out above the shouts of the crowd and the throbbing of the *goma* drums. When I stepped forward Bruce laughed his barbaric laugh and my dog remarked *How barbaric he is,* then growled. I went up to Bruce, growling too, and the referee looked at Bruce who said *OK!* and smiled with his wolfish teeth and, as everyone knows, dogs don't like wolves.

Bruce began dancing his little dance, leaping and crouching and circling around me laughing and the crowd was laughing too, I heard shouts of *The nutjob! The nutjob!* But then something incredible happened, Bosco came up close to me and entered me. Into one leg, then the other, into one arm, then the other, into my head, then my heart and I became very big, a big dog with close-cropped fur and dark patches and I pounced on him suddenly making a prodigious spring as he went on laughing and he toppled over and my dog arms punched his head while my dog legs held him gripped and my dog heart was barking and my dog head was yelling.

The cry that welled up from my guts awakened something within me and it struck me that it was the same thing that was awakened when I was reading my book, when I thought about my house, when I dreamed of Marie. I saw Bruce's face and my foot on his throat and I knew I needed to disappear.

I ran, went to fetch my bag that I'd hidden beside the water meter, then remembered the gun. I'd got down the hillside before they could find me and I ran across the Kaweni road

136

and along beside the mangrove swamp and got onto the ferry without a backward glance and even as I sat there on the wooden benches I was still running in my head, in my heart. I didn't watch Grande-Terre receding, I didn't look to see if Gaza was changing into a monster, I came back here, I slept on the ping-pong table and before sunrise I walked as far as Lake Dziani to remind myself of how it was in the old days when I used to go there with Marie, and then Bruce appeared among the trees and I didn't want any more of all that, I didn't want to be down on the ground again, I didn't want to be mutilated again, I didn't want to be raped again and I took out the gun and I barely squeezed the trigger.

Olivier

In the garden by my little house there are pink hibiscus with red hearts and yellow pistils, a frangipani tree with velvety white flowers, allamandas that produce flowers as yellow as the sun all through the year, and fuchsia bougainvillea climbing up one panel of the boundary wall. I spend hours here, trimming, pruning, nurturing, removing the insects one by one, nurturing, feeding, watering, protecting. I spend a part of my life here, looking, marveling at the colors, the shapes, the perfumes, like a freshly arrived tourist. I bow down in awe before the fineness of the veins in the flowers and the softness of their petals, I watch butterflies, hummingbirds, bulbuls, and many species of songbird. Every morning when I walk in after a night on duty, I stand motionless in this garden and feel as if I'm taking root here, taking on the colors of these intense, unchanging hues and every morning I contrive to feel as if I belong a little, just a very little, to this land.

But this afternoon when I finally come home after twenty hours on duty, this garden seems to me a fraud, a cliché, a picture postcard for tourists. I go into the garden and beneath the blazing metallic sunlight I wait to be moved, I wait to be washed clean, I scan the flowers with my eyes, I listen for the birds, I wait to be calmed, I wait to be comforted.

Bruce's body has been taken to the mortuary at the Dzaoudzi hospital. It's not really a mortuary, it's a solid structure separate from the main buildings. Three air conditioners turned up to the maximum keep the room cold. Bacar and I did our best to avoid news of the affair spreading but when we came back down the hill with Bruce's body wrapped in a sheet there was already a crowd around the emergency services vehicles. People were boldly calling out *Who's that?* and Bacar snapped back *It's a tourist.* Just now a reporter from Mayotte's daily newspaper called the police station to ask for information about the body found near the lake. I don't know how long we'll be able to keep it quiet, act as if nothing had happened, act as if it were just a trivial incident.

I think about Moïse and about Bruce, and suddenly the unbearable thought hits me that they look like one another. The same build, the same shaped head, the same full lips, both with lean faces. I was once told that they're all cousins here and that the blood that flows into the ocean passes back into the sand, the land, feeds the rivers and the plantations. My skin's burning, my head's about to burst and I look at my flowers. Are they so lovely because they feed on flesh? Are they so vivid because they gorge on blood? My heart begins racing and to stop myself from going mad, before the flowers change into hands, the branches into arms, the tree trunks into bodies, I grasp the spade and strike down the red, smash the velvety white, beat down the sun yellow, kill the pink, silence the fuchsia bougainvillea forever.

"Olivier! Olivier!"

It's Bacar. He has the keys to my house, as I have his. When I go on vacation he calls every day to water my plants and to check that I haven't been burglarized. When he's away I go to his house.

He gives me such a sad look that it makes me want to weep. What are we going to do, Bacar? I want to ask him. What can we do to fix it all?

He hands me a sheet of paper and says, "The chief constable tried to call you several times but you didn't pick up. The boy has to be driven to the court."

"Now?"

"Yes, now. Hold on, take a look."

"What's this?"

"It's an article that appeared on the internet an hour ago."

The piece was several lines long and had been posted at 3:55 p.m. I read it as I followed Bacar to the car.

YOUTH KILLED BY FIREARM THIS MORNING

A youth was killed by a firearm on Petite-Terre this morning. Our sources inform us that it was a certain Bruce, a gang leader known to the inhabitants of Gaza, the shantytown on the outskirts of the capital city, Mamoudzou. This is the first crime involving firearms in France's most recently created *département*. Our sources inform us that Bruce was a minor.

For several years Mayotte has experienced an alarming increase in violence and delinquency. France's 101st *département*, known as the isle of perfumes or the lagoon island, also faces pressure from constant immigration from the Comoros Islands, Madagascar, and even some African countries. Almost 20,000 people were deported in 2014 but the *kwassa-kwassas* still arrive daily on the shores of Mayotte, and 597 landings were intercepted in 2014. It has been estimated that in France's 101st *département* some 3000 unaccompanied minors have now been living as outlaws for a sustained period of time.   S.R.

I looked at Bacar, who was having trouble starting his car. He was shaking.

"We must get him away, this youngster. He's just a kid."

"Yes, the prefect recommends that he be transferred to Réunion, but first he has to be brought before the magistrate, and the court's in Mamoudzou."

"We'd better get there fast, before the news spreads."

Bacar turned to me and I knew what he was about to say, I knew what my friend of twenty years was thinking. At this very moment the whole of Gaza knew about Bruce's death and was preparing for war. I folded up the sheet of paper, the car drove off and for the second time that day I closed my eyes and prayed.

Bruce

Don't try to get some shut-eye, Mo, don't chill, don't close
your eyes, it's not over yet. They're looking for you and if
they have to search every nook and cranny in this country to
hunt you down they're up for it. The noise you can hear that
sounds like empty barrels rolling along, or else like thunder in
January, well if you think it's that, you're wrong. Get ready,
Mo-ïse it's not over yet. You ran here like a scaredy-cat after
gunning me down, they've put you in this cell nice and safe,
nice and cool, but you can hear that noise, can't you, and feel
the earth shaking? Nothing's going to save you from Gaza's
rage, not the *muzungus*, not the walls, not the sea, not the
djinn, not the law, not the firemen, not Stéphane, not books,
not your rotten old dog whose head I kicked to pieces, not
your kid's stories about boys and rivers.

Hear my country's roar, hear Gaza's rage, hear how it
creeps and raps its way toward us, hear that nigga music, feel
the glowing embers against your scarred face. Look, Mo,
take a look with your cursed djinn's eye. They're coming for
revenge.

They're coming for you.

Marie

You must believe me. Here, I'm a memory rising to the surface, a shadow lengthening at dusk, the misty corner of an eye. I still turn in the wind, but I no longer burn in the sun. Hours and days and years pass down this same road, with no colors, no contours, no light. Lies and dreams no longer exist. Just life subsists and the hell of others.

I can hear the clamor and fury swelling in the lanes and alleyways of Gaza, I can feel the ground shaking as all those feet pound the earth in its streets. Something's coming near but my son doesn't know it yet.

I watch Moïse lying on the ground in his cell. He's tired from his journey to hell which began the day I collapsed onto our kitchen floor. And the other boy, the one who could never be still, the one who couldn't believe he was dead, wants to get away but he can't. He hasn't yet learned that it's not his decision.

The silence around Moïse is doing him good, he's looking through the window at the unmoving blue sky and remembering the word he was trying to find just now, trompe l'oeil. He closes his eyes.

His thoughts are dancing around like mayflies at the end

of the southern winter. He's imagining the moment when he'll be able to slip his arms through the straps of his rucksack again, give a little hitch of his hips to hoist it up, tighten the buckles and feel its familiar weight on his back. He's thinking about the way the policeman spoke to him just now. He's wondering how long he's going to stay in this big, square cell. He tells himself he could stay here for weeks, even years, and he'd be content with that blue sky, with this cool concrete floor.

One thought is followed by another. He thinks about me and sees me in his mind's eye at Nassuf's restaurant one evening, in my blue-and-green silk scarf. Right there, in front of our steaming plates of fish in coconut milk, I'm laughing and saying *But to be a coral planter's not a profession!* The memory of me, of us two together, stops his shaking. He smiles very slightly and the scar running across his face barely moves. His stomach rumbles but he has no desire to eat, he now prefers to withstand his own body, to feel independent of it. When he thinks about the juvenile magistrate who'll be seeing him soon now, or tomorrow, he pictures himself in an elegant office opposite a woman whose face looks like mine.

Outside, suddenly, the wheels of a vehicle squeal on the gravel. Car doors slam. There are hurried, impatient shouts.

Moïse's thoughts slow down, I can see their contours, huddling back, closing in on themselves, withering with fear, turning into heavy marbles and plummeting silently to the ground one by one.

Moïse gets up and stands in the elongated rectangle of light. He closes his fingers around an imaginary pistol, points his index finger at his own brow and says *Bang*.

Moïse

The cop takes me by the right arm, the fireman by the left, and they pick me up as if I were nothing but a bit of dry wood, hollow inside. As my feet leave the ground they pause for a microsecond and look at one another in surprise, as if they were expecting something else, for me to be heavier, for me to protest, I don't know.

I want to ask the cop if I can retrieve my rucksack but he's red in the face and sweating heavily. His shirt is soaking and at intervals the sugary, acrid smell of him reaches my nostrils. The fireman, in uniform, settles in at the wheel but before driving off he looks at me in the driving mirror. The look he gives me is so gentle that it's unbearable. I look down.

"Moïse?"

"Yes."

"We're taking you to see the magistrate but don't get out of the car until we reach the courthouse. Even on the ferry we'll stay in the car, do you understand? Otherwise I'll put the cuffs on you."

"They're looking for me, aren't they?"

The cop doesn't answer, but just slaps the driver's seat with the flat of his hand. The fireman drives off at full tilt.

146

Inside the red 4x4 I do what I've so often done in Gaza. I sit with my knees pressed together, my hands between my thighs, my head sunk into my shoulders, staring at my feet. I inhale deeply, holding my breath as long as possible, breathing out slowly. Making myself small, as small as a useless pebble.

I like to think that if I'd looked out I'd be seeing all the things I used to see when I lived on Petite-Terre with Marie and Bosco. The almost perfect view of the airport to the left, just after the Judo Club, the elegant sidewalks neatly lining the road that always seems newly resurfaced, black and smooth, the torrent of fabrics of all colors hanging from the verandas of the little corrugated iron shops, the smell of fries from Maoré Burger, the dry, closely mown lawn in front of the airport, the palm trees in the wind, the white-and-blue aircraft against the horizon. Or maybe the pizza van beside the post office with its permanent advertisement, "Buy four pizzas get one free," the dense bougainvilleas at the entrance to the Chinese restaurant, and the market women reclining beside their displays of tomatoes and bananas. I like to think that for one last time I'd catch sight of my friend Moussa coming back from school, impatient to listen to his *mgodro* music and to shake his buttocks. In Labbatoir there'd be the usual old men, the *bacocos* who don't speak a word of French, tucked away in odd corners selling jasmine flowers for one euro a bunch. In the little bay beside the fishermen's jetty there'd certainly be children and in the car park the fishermen would be using bits of cardboard to chase away the flies from the treasure of their catch: tread-fins, parrot fish, bonitos, long-fin tuna.

As the car gathered speed along the boulevard des Crabes, I imagined the wind on my face, the sea, blue and green on both sides of the road, beating against the black heart of the rocks.

At this time of the afternoon there'd certainly already be blue smoke from the grilled meat stalls and dozens of taxis in the car park by the landing stage. In the distance, if I'd been able to look out, I'd have seen the ferry approaching. And then I'd have waited, counting the way Marie used to inside her hand, on the thick flesh of her finger joints, the seconds that elapsed before hearing the ferry's siren, one-two-three little finger, four-five-six ring finger . . .

On the ferry, Olivier, the cop, tells me to keep my head down which isn't a problem for me. Beneath my feet I can feel the throbbing of the boat's engine and the backwash of the waves. In the depths of the water I picture the invisible furrows left by the dugongs and coelacanths and, deeper still, those creatures with huge mouths and teeth shaped like claws that only live in the ocean's darkness. The pleasant rocking motion made me stop thinking about Bruce, about Marie, about Bosco, about the house. I thought about a boy born fifteen years ago on one of the Comoros Islands who could have had a different life if he'd been born with two dark eyes. I wondered what he could have done, that boy, to break free from his chains, to avoid that path he'd started on of violence, ignorance, and revulsion. I wondered if the truth wasn't that he was done for before he'd even begun, that boy, and along with him, all those other boys and girls, born, like him, in the wrong place at the wrong time.

I thought about those long minutes spent swimming in the bay at Bandrakouni, the velvety water that had taken me in its arms gently, gently. Maybe I should have gone on swimming that day, thrusting with my arms and legs, the way I still know how to do, swimming, swimming until I came to a land that would accept a boy like me.

The siren sounds as we approach the bay of Mamoudzou and the ferry comes alongside. The fireman drives off and slowly the car moves down the creaking gangway, then up onto the jetty. Olivier says to me *That's right, keep your head down.* I give him a sidelong glance, he looks uneasy but smiles and whispers *Everything's OK Moïse.* Then he gestures and holds out his hand so that it lies across the part of my face that's scarred. His skin's cool against my scar which no longer feels tight, it no longer exists at all and I'd like him to keep his hand against my face a little longer, just a little longer. The vehicle drives forward in the line of cars, it's heading down the laterite track which runs beside the market which soon joins the main road. Over to the right lies Gaza, along to the left lie the magistrate's court, then the towns of Passamainti, Dembeni, Bandrele, Kani-Kéli. And all the while Olivier has kept his hand there, maybe I'm leaning my head gently against his palm the way Bosco used to do when he wanted me to go on stroking him, but all at once he has a sharp intake of breath, withdraws his hand from my face and says *Holy shit, what the fuck's going on?* But I know.

I've stopped keeping my head down. I'm looking out of the window because when the moment comes and it's all over, you've got no choice. What I can see is unreal and, in all its unreality, its ponderousness, depth, and darkness, it is becoming magnificent.

To my right, the mangrove swamp seems to be stirring, quivering, moving. Dozens of children are emerging from between the mangrove trees and their green leaves and tangled branches along that stretch of sand-earth-and-sea. They aren't running, they're not hurrying, it's as if they're in slow motion. They're wearing shorts and T-shirts, their legs are the color of ash, their mouths are shut but they have sticks in their hands. All along the road that leads to Gaza barrels are rolling toward us with a rumbling sound and behind each barrel there are children and young men. In the gullies on the red hill facing us other children are waiting. To the left, coming down from place Mariage and the steps of the administrative building, above which the blue, white, and red flag is flying, boys with bare chests are advancing toward us. They have machetes in their hands and they, too, are walking slowly.

There is a brief moment of silence when in the yellow afternoon light all that is moving is the mangrove swamp, the earth, the hill and the children of Mayotte.

The cars begin hooting, some of them are trying to get out of the line of traffic, others try to back away. Olivier and the fireman start yelling into their phones. Their words reach my ears in jerky bursts, *reinforcements, kids, Gaza, rioters, war* and I only half understand their words. I'm outside my body, I'm in the car, but I'm also outside it, I don't know if it's fear that does this or if madness is taking possession of me.

Soon this moving noose that surrounds us begins to open its mouth and only one sound, one single syllable emerges from its giant mouth, *MO!* And the sticks beat the ground, *MO!* And the machetes slice the air, *MO!* And the children wave their fists that are clutching stones, *MO!* The noose unfurls around us like some monstrous octopus.

I don't know what comes over me, it's like an impulse, as deep as the ocean, not to give in, not to march to their tune, this time, and while the acrid and sugary stench from Olivier fills the passenger compartment, and the fireman is reaching under his seat for a big stick, I leap out of the car. I hear Olivier's voice yelling, *Moïse,* but I don't look back. Behind me the mangrove swamp, the hillside and the whole road that leads to Gaza all explode at the same time with a monumental din.

MO! they all yell.

I don't stop, tonight it's war, tonight it's the wolves' banquet and no one could protect me from this pack. I bob and weave between the cars, I see stunned faces behind the windows, people hiding between rocks but I don't stop, I'm running toward the sea that brought me here. As long as my feet are pounding the earth I'm not afraid, as long as I can feel the hot, salty breeze lashing my face, hear the fury behind me, no, it's not like it was before when everything would shrivel up inside me, when I no longer knew who I was and what my name was. No, as long as I'm heading for the ocean, I'm no longer afraid.

My name's Moïse, I'm fifteen years old, and I'm alive.

I see the jetty and I speed up, I'm thrust onward by the *chacal's* breath of the pack, by my desire to wash away that whole shitty life, I'm thinking about Marie, I'm thinking about Bosco and about Gatzo and Pascalet and it seems to me that they're here, running beside me, encouraging me, carrying me along. I can feel the ground changing, it's no longer earth but the jetty's hard cement beneath my feet. I can't see the others, I'm no longer scared of them, armed with their machetes, their cudgels, and their stones. I soon get to the end but I'm not afraid, this magnificent, shining blue, this blue that maybe only exists here in this ocean, is calling me. Without pausing I do what all the children on Mayotte do at least once in their lives, I launch my body off the end of the jetty, my chest swells, my legs and arms fly up. I dive into Mamoudzou's harbor, I cleave the ocean with my supple, living body, and I don't resurface.

NATHACHA APPANAH was born in Mauritius in 1973, and she was brought up there, eventually working as a journalist, before moving to France in 1998. Her previous novels include *The Last Brother* and *Waiting for Tomorrow*. *Tropic of Violence* was the winner of the Prix Femina des Lycéens in 2016, as well as seven other literary awards.

GEOFFREY STRACHAN is the translator of the novels of Andreï Makine and Jérôme Ferrari, as well as of Nathacha Appanah's *The Last Brother* and *Waiting for Tomorrow*. He was awarded the Scott Moncrieff Prize for his translation of *Le Testament Français*.

The text of *Tropic of Violence* is set in Haarlemmer. Book design by Libanus Press. Composition by Bookmobile Design and Digital Publisher Services, Minneapolis, Minnesota. Manufactured by McNaughton & Gunn on acid-free, 30 percent postconsumer wastepaper.